TALES OF THE KING

THE JOURNEY WITH THE
GOLDEN BOOK

Also by Lela Gilbert

Tales of the King, Book One: *The Quest for the Silver Castle*
Prelude
Interlude
Reprise

TALES OF THE KING

THE JOURNEY WITH THE GOLDEN BOOK

LELA GILBERT

HARVEST HOUSE PUBLISHERS
Eugene, Oregon 97402

Tales of the King, Book Two: The Journey with the Golden book

Copyright © 1993 by Harvest House Publishers
Eugene, Oregon 97402

Library of Congress Cataloging-in-Publication Data

Gilbert, Lela.
     The journey with the golden book / Lela Gilbert.
         p. cm. — (Tales of the king ; bk.)
     Summary: In this allegory, two children are sent by the King to share stories of his love with people across the land and to fight against the Six Cruel Kings. Sequel to "The Quest for the Silver Castle."
     ISBN 1-56507-105-0
     [1. Kings, queens, rulers, etc.—Fiction. 2. Adventure and adventures—Fiction. 3. Christian life — Fiction.] I. Title.
II. Series: Gilbert, Lela. Tales of the king ; bk.
PZ7.G3748Jo 1993
[Fic]— dc20   92-44364
                                               CIP
                                               AC

For Amanda Aikman

Contents

1

The King's Orders

IT WAS NEARLY WINTER in the village called Place-Beneath-the-Castle, and a frosty wind curled itself around the necks and ears of the two children sitting together in the apple grove by the crossroads. It was late in the day, and they shivered a little as they talked. The boy turned up the collar of his coat. The girl pulled the hood of her woolen cape up over her long hair. But they exchanged warm smiles as they savored the sweet red fruit and talked over their plans.

Arlen and Theodora were friends for several very good reasons.

They were friends because they were nearly the same age and lived close to each other.

They were good friends because they were interested in any number of the same things.

But they were especially dear and inseparable friends because they had just been through an extraordinary experience together—something amazing, something awesome, something never to be forgotten. Even now, the memory of it was enough to still their earnest conversation into a delighted silence.

For not many days before, Arlen and Theodora had found the King of the land. Or had he found them? At any rate, their difficult and dangerous journey had ended at the very castle whose silver turrets they had seen glinting elusively in the far-off mountain peaks. And within its shining ramparts they'd met a tenderhearted monarch who, they discovered, had dearly loved them all their lives and wanted them to love him, too. Arlen and Theodora had stared in awe at the rooms and halls of his magnificent residence. They had shared a lavish banquet with their monarch. They had received from him a glorious gift.

And with the gift, the King had assigned to Arlen and Theodora an important and challenging task.

He had placed in the children's hands a wonderful book called *Tales of the King*—a golden volume with beautiful parchment pages. Best of all, whenever the children looked inside its cover, captivating stories were acted out in life like reality right before their eyes!

"I'm sending the two of you together to take this book to the people of my kingdom," the King had explained. "Those who believe in my existence will be astounded to watch page after page come to life, just as you have done. As the stories about my love unfold, they will come to realize what you now realize—that I know, and I feel, and I understand. Perhaps they'll learn to love me, just as you have done.

"But those who don't believe in my existence," he warned, "will see only words...and boring, empty words at that."

Shortly thereafter, book firmly in hand, the children had sadly said goodbye to the King. Then they had been magically whisked across a cold autumn sky and delivered, safe and sound, to Theodora's cottage, arriving just moments after the girl's mother had given birth to a brand-new baby boy. And Arlen had blushed with pleasure when he was told the tiny infant's name—Arlen Theodore.

The story of how Arlen had helped save the life of Theodora's father, Burke Brighton, is found in another book. But it should be mentioned that it was Burke himself who firmly insisted on naming the baby after his daughter's courageous, loyal friend.

"I want him to be just like you as he grows up, son.

I'm especially proud of you, you know. And grateful to you, too, by the way." Burke had beamed as he hugged the boy's shoulders.

Arlen lived with his grandmother, not far from the Brighton farm. Upon his return, he had told her as much as he thought she would understand about his journey with Theodora. How she had glowed with pleasure when Arlen described the King's many kindnesses to her grandson! But the boy had left out some sad facts about his own father, Granma's only son—facts which would have served to grieve her heart.

Theodora had shown her family the glorious book and had breathlessly recounted the miraculous adventure she and Arlen had shared. She couldn't help but notice that some of her brothers and sisters had been captivated by its pages, while others had either glanced at it politely or hadn't looked at all.

But now, all that was behind them. By now, traveling clothes had been laundered, mended, and pressed. Chores had been resumed, and life had returned to normal. Or almost to normal. For one thing was all-too-evident to everyone who knew Arlen and Theodora. Neither child would ever be the same again. They talked of little else but the generous, loving man who lived in the faraway castle. And though they were obviously glad to be home, something new was in their faces. Was it a strange longing? A sweet sadness? Nobody could be sure, but people agreed that Arlen and Theodora were most certainly different.

They felt different, too. They were more patient. More caring. More helpful. But oh, how they missed their new friend! Now that they had met him, they yearned to spend every moment with him.

The next best thing they could do, of course, would be to follow his orders about the book. They could only hope that they might have the opportunity to meet up with him again in the process.

By now Arlen had made extensive plans for the two of them to take the King's book around the village of Place. The boy had also drawn up a detailed map of the neighboring village, Kingsdale.

"See?" he explained to Theodora. "We'll mark off each cottage and shop we visit, until we've shown the book to everyone there. After that we'll move on."

With even more complex maps and sketches, Arlen planned to conclude their mission by taking the golden book to the City of Bells, his original home, where his wicked father and the Six Cruel Kings lived. It was to that city that the true King had promised to return someday.

From Arlen's point of view, their future course was set. The boy had already spent many hours devising maps and planning strategies; now he felt it was about time he and Theodora began their task of following the King's orders. He was growing restless. Even now, as he tossed away his apple core, he began pulling his carefully folded maps and notes out of his pocket.

Theodora watched him with thoughtful eyes. "What if the King has a different idea about how he wants us to take his book around the kingdom? What if he doesn't want us to begin the work in Place at all?"

"What do you mean?" Arlen stared at his friend in bewilderment.

"Well, I know how hard you've worked at your maps and all, Arlen, but I just wonder if he might have some other plan in mind..."

"If he did, he didn't mention it to me!" Arlen unsuccessfully tried to keep a tone of frustration out of his voice.

"No, he didn't mention it," Theodora was afraid she had offended her friend. "And I know how closely you were listening, Arlen."

"I was! I wrote it all down, too. No, he didn't say a thing about where we should go. Or how we should get there. I think we'd best just go ahead with my idea."

Maybe that's why he chose me to go, because I'm such a good planner. Arlen kept the thought silent, priding himself in the fact that Theodora wasn't really much of a planner at all.

Nor was Theodora an argumentative child. And she wasn't really sure just why she'd questioned Arlen's elaborate preparations. She was very proud of her friend,

admiring his skill and his thoroughness and the sharp
intelligence that shone in his clear, blue eyes.

Her own brown eyes, by contrast, tended to be soft
with dreams. She rarely considered the order of her days
because she enjoyed nothing more than surprises. That's
probably why she often found herself catching her breath
in amazement at the many marvelous things that always
seemed to be happening around her.

Maybe that's why he chose me to go, Theodora
thought to herself. *Because I like surprises.* She found
herself wondering if Arlen didn't find surprises annoying
when they interrupted his plans.

There it was again—that same thought. Theodora
couldn't say just why, but something was bothering her a
bit about Arlen's plans. Was it because the two of them
had seen evidence of a wonderfully bigger world while
they were guests in the King's castle? The King appeared
to reign over countless other realms besides the one they
knew. And even within their own part of his kingdom, it
seemed there might be villages they'd never heard about.
Cities they'd never dreamed of. People they'd never
imagined.

These ideas excited the girl and made her soft eyes
shine. Would the King's orders provide more thrilling
adventures than they'd already had? Suppose they
discovered new lands and fantastic new creatures!
Suppose the King himself joined them! Suppose...

Suddenly a noise stirred the air around them. It

sounded like a flood, or a rushing river, or a waterfall. But it was a voice, and by now a familiar one. At first it spoke just three words.

"Not now, Arlen."

Arlen looked up, puzzled and delighted beyond measure at the sight of one of the King's messengers, a rainbow-hued being who shimmered and shone with every color. It had been just such a creature that had borne the children high above the winds on their homeward journey days before. Even though that remarkable experience was still fresh in Arlen's young mind, the sight of the rainbow being lifted his spirits with joyful recollections of the beloved King.

"Not now?" Arlen softly echoed.

"Later, Arlen. Your plans are good ones, but there are other places you must go. The familiar will wait; the unknown will come first. You must offer the King's book to men and women, boys and girls whom you know nothing about. They have a greater need."

"But who are they?" Theodora's face was rosy with anticipation, and her words sounded almost like a whisper. "Who are they?" She repeated the question in a louder voice, just in case the messenger hadn't heard.

"You will learn soon enough. But prepare yourselves. Those whom you meet will make you both happy and sad. They will bring you both laughter and tears. They will embrace you, and they will send you away. Be strong. Be brave. Share your thoughts, and do not leave each other, whatever you do."

"So I should always stay with Theodora?" Arlen queried, concerned as always about getting his instructions correct.

"The King has chosen for you to take his message together. If either of you is absent, your journey will be far more difficult, and the message will be incomplete."

With that, the rainbow being shimmered into nothingness, and the two children stared at each other in wonder.

Finally Arlen spoke. "How did you know my idea wasn't so good?" He might have felt a twinge of spitefulness toward his friend if he hadn't just been told that the two of them would do well to share their thoughts. Besides, in the course of their adventures, Arlen had come to suspect that Theodora often viewed the world in much the same way that the King did.

"Oh, please don't feel bad, Arlen!" Theodora brushed her long, wind-tangled hair out of her eyes. "The messenger didn't say your plan wasn't a good one. In fact, he said it was!" The girl patted her friend's hand and smiled at him. "You just got a bit ahead of the King, that's all. Sometimes—well sometimes, he seems unusually particular about *when* things happen!"

Arlen nodded. "Well, it's true that he always seems to send his messengers just when we need them."

"Yes, he does." Then Theodora sighed softly, her

chin resting on her knees. "But I do sometimes wish they'd tell us more! I can't help but wonder how we'll know where to go with the book. And how long before we begin. And how we'll get there, and how we'll find our way..."

Theodora's questions faded into silence as she began to think and to dream and to wonder.

"I don't know," Arlen shrugged, "But it seems to me that we're going to have to find our way without a map—at least this time." With a sigh he tucked his notes and drawings back into his pocket. "I'm freezing, aren't you? Let's go home."

Theodora nodded, stood up, and lifted her gaze toward the craggy mountains where she knew the castle's turrets were obscured. She waved and laughed. "Hello, King? Can you see us? I hope you're listening, because we can't do what you told us to do unless you tell us how!"

"Otherwise, we're never going to find our way," added Arlen, who was feeling a trifle glum in spite of himself.

Without another word, the two children began to walk back toward their cottages. Beyond them, on a distant mountaintop, a glimmer of silver caught the last light of day and winked brightly between drifting clouds.

2

Two Dreamers

BEYOND THEODORA'S window, clouds and stars were strewn across the cold sky. She pulled on her long, white nightgown, brushed out her hair, and gladly crawled under her quilt. At first, she fixed her eyes upon a windowpane and watched for the rising moon, vaguely wishing she could somehow talk to the King. But before long her lids grew heavy, and she drifted off into warm slumbers.

The early hours of her sleep were silent and deep,

uninterrupted by dreams. Then, gradually, Theodora entered some unknown time, some unfamiliar place. There she found herself abruptly confronted by a heavy-set, peculiarly dressed man. His garments appeared to be robes of royalty, ornate and lavish. But looking more closely, Theodora noticed their excessively bright purple color. Their metallic decorations looked artificial and even a little garish.

In the dream, Theodora realized that the man was supposed to be a king or a prince or some sort of an imperial personage. "Your costume is very...well, it's quite impressive," she said politely to the man.

"Yes," he answered, pleased by her compliment, "and isn't my crown beautiful?"

Theodora stared and squinted and shook her head. "But where is your crown, sir?"

"Why, it's on my head, child. Can't you see it?"

"Pardon me, but you must have lost it somewhere. There is no crown on your head at all."

"Of course there's a crown! I'm a special heir to the kingdom, and I always wear my crown." The oddly garbed man put his hand to the top of his head and appeared to be fingering something there. "See? It's right here! Silly girl, why are you teasing me?"

Theodora again looked at the man's clothing. The cloth was so strangely vivid. Yet the gold braid on his robe shone with barely a dull luster, and the jewels that studded his cuffs and collar hardly sparkled at all. Again she looked at his head.

"Sir, I really think you are mistaken about your crown. It's simply not there!"

"You are a rude girl! How dare you insult me with your foolish jokes? I think you are jealous of my crown. That must be it. You don't have one, so you're pretending I don't have one either!"

The man and Theodora stared at each other silently for a moment. Then he spoke again in a firm, demanding voice. "Just bring the book, foolish girl. Forget the business of the crown and bring the book. Everyone in King's Common is expecting to see it, and to see it soon."

With that, the haughty man turned and walked away from Theodora. And at that moment she awoke, sitting bolt upright in bed. What an unusual and disturbing dream!

Just bring the book...everyone in King's Common is expecting to see it... Theodora tried to recapture the dream in her memory. She recalled the man's gaudy costume and unexplainably crownless head. And, although his face was already a blur in her mind, she could still hear the disdain in his voice.

"I've got to remember to tell Arlen everything tomorrow," she muttered to herself.

"Mmmph? What?" Theodora's sister Geraldine stirred in her nearby bed.

"Oh, sorry! It's nothing...go back to sleep,"

Theodora said apologetically, snuggling back under her quilt.

Bring the book. King's Common. Everyone is expecting to see it... She repeated the words to herself until she fell asleep again, hoping against hope that she wouldn't forget a thing she'd seen or heard in the dream.

Meanwhile, past tidy fields and stone fences, in the loft of Granma's house, Arlen's tousled blonde head lay upon his pillow. He was fast asleep, and no dreams disturbed his slumbers.

Then, unexpectedly, he found himself standing in the presence of a gaunt, haggard woman. She was dressed from head to toe in rags—brown and tan and gray tatters. Beneath her eyes were deep shadows. Her arms and neck were far too thin. But upon her head was the most glorious crown Arlen could ever have imagined.

It was fashioned of gold, delicately woven into a fine pattern of squares, and each square was studded with a tiny, blazing jewel. Rubies, diamonds, emeralds, and sapphires shimmered like lacework above the weary woman's face.

"You must come to us," she whispered, looking back over her shoulder in fear, as if someone might be listening. "You must bring the book! We have to see it!"

Shocked as he was by her ragged attire, Arlen still couldn't take his eyes off the glittering crown. "Yes, of course we'll bring the book. But your crown...it's so beautiful!"

"Crown?" The woman looked at him as if he were mad. Again, she whispered hoarsely and looked furtively behind her. "Crown? Why do you mock me?" Tears flooded her eyes.

Arlen stared at the woman in disbelief. "I'm not mocking you at all, ma'am. Surely you know that there is a splendid crown on your head. It's absolutely ablaze with jewels!"

"You are so unkind..." The woman's fingers dug into her matted black hair. Somehow, she couldn't feel the crown's surface. She sobbed aloud and looked at Arlen in dismay. "I don't see why you'd laugh at someone so miserable."

"Forgive me, I...I guess I must have imagined it." The crown continued to twinkle in Arlen's eyes, but he pretended not to see it.

"Listen, all we want from you is the book. Bring it to us. Please! Bring the book to Mansfield, and quickly. Things are growing worse every day. And whatever you do, don't mock us, lad. We are suffering enough as it is. Don't mock us with your talk of crowns."

The poor woman looked around fearfully one more time, then turned and fled. The last thing Arlen saw was the sparkle of her dazzling crown as she vanished into the depths of his dream.

Suddenly awake, Arlen threw back his bedcovers, rushed to his table, and lit a candle. *I've got to write all this down so I won't forget to tell Theodora any of it. This must be our new plan! Let's see...Mansfield...bring the book...*

Arlen made note of all he had seen and heard. He tried his best to describe the woman and her wretched appearance. *I wonder what the crown was all about. And the rags. What a very strange dream it was!*

After having satisfied himself that he'd recorded all he could recall, Arlen crawled back into his bed. The next thing he knew, Granma was shaking him. "Arlen, you've slept well past daybreak! Aren't you going to do your chores today? Have you been up drawing more maps? Bless you, child, keep at it and you'll make a living as a mapmaker someday!"

Arlen was bone tired. He could hardly move his sleep-heavy legs to the side of the bed. He sat rubbing his eyes for several seconds before he finally stood up. Then he noticed scattered papers on the table, and his energy quickly returned as he read the details of his dream.

"I've got to talk to Theodora as soon as possible!" he whispered to himself. "I wonder if she's ever heard of a place called Mansfield. I'm sure I haven't, but then I haven't lived here very long, either."

Arlen rushed through his morning responsibilities. He had just finished when he saw Theodora running toward him, an expression of great urgency on her face.

"Arlen!" she waved. "I've got to talk to you!"

"I've got to talk to you, too. Come inside! You see, I had the strangest dream..."

"A dream? So did I! I had a dream, too! Was yours about a man with a king's costume but no crown?"

Arlen looked at her strangely and answered slowly. "No, my dream was about a woman in rags. And she wore the most beautiful crown you could ever imagine."

"A woman with a crown? The man in my dream thought he was wearing a crown, but he wasn't."

"The woman in my dream didn't know she was wearing a crown, but she was."

Words tumbled over words, thoughts piled atop other thoughts as they shared their stories. But before long they had carefully written down the two aspects of the order that seemed to be most important:

> Bring the book to Manfsield.
> Bring the book to King's Common.

"Are you familiar with either place, Theodora? You've lived here all your life, haven't you?"

Theodora shook her head without a word, a frown creasing her forehead. "Let's ask my father. Maybe he knows."

"Where are you two going?" Granma's friendly smile stopped them. They looked at each other, and Arlen spoke hesitantly, "Granma, have you ever heard of a place called Mansfield or a place called King's Common?"

Granma looked perplexed. "Mansfield. Mansfield.

Hmmm...It seems I once heard the name at your father's house in the City of Bells. Some friend of your father's... What was it now? Oh, my, yes. Silly man—he had changed the name of a village from Kingsfield to Mansfield. Who knows why?"

"Do you remember where the village was?"

"Oh, I have no idea, Arlen. You know how your father is. He's not one to make small talk about his friends' affairs."

"And for good reason, I might add!" Arlen muttered to himself as he and Theodora set out for the Brighton farm. When they found Theodora's father, they quickly asked him about the two villages. He scratched his head and tried to remember something long past and nearly forgotten.

"King's Common? I seem to recall a group of people dressed in odd clothing who came to our cottage some years ago. They were from a place with a name similar to that. Maybe it was King's Common..." Then Burke Brighton's face brightened as his memory cleared. "Yes! King's Common *was* the name of the place. Anyway, they said they were special heirs in the kingdom, and they wanted to sell us some books explaining why. We had no money, so they went away."

Burke studied the children's earnest faces fondly. "Now what is it you children are up to?" Smiling, he touched Theodora's cheek with his rough hand. "Dreaming again, little one?"

She looked at him, wondering just what he meant. "Yes, Father. I mean, no, Father. What I mean is, I don't think it will be much longer before Arlen and I take the King's book out into the kingdom..."

"I don't think it will be much longer, either, Theodora. And when you're ready to go, please let me know if I can help. You know, I promised the King I'd be his man in Place. And the least I can do is to help you fulfill his orders."

The children slowly wended their way down the road, absently heading toward the apple grove. Arlen was trying to absorb everything they had learned.

"Mansfield used to be Kingsfield. And King's Common is a village of people who are special heirs of the King. Is that what you understood?"

"Yes, I think so. You know, Arlen, if it was one of your father's friends who changed the name from Kingsfield to Mansfield, you can well imagine why! I'll bet there's more to that story than what your Granma heard!"

"Oh, yes. There's no doubt in my mind but that the Six Cruel Kings had their bony fingers right in the middle of it! Mansfield, indeed!"

Theodora smiled at a new thought. "On the other hand, it would be fun to meet people who were special heirs of the King, don't you think? Maybe they're relatives of his! They might be just like him!"

"The man in your dream didn't sound much like the King to me."

"No." Theodora shivered suddenly. "No, he couldn't have been less like him, really. I wonder what it all means, Arlen."

The boy and girl absently sat down at their usual meeting place. The apple grove was very still. Not a breeze stirred, and not even the trill of a birdsong broke the silence.

"And I wonder how we're going to find those villages. No map. No directions. No guide." Arlen sighed, chin in hand, unable to conceive of a possible solution.

Just then a clatter of hoofbeats interrupted their worries. A man on horseback rode up, leading a second horse behind him. He was dressed in dusty, well-worn riding clothes, and a hat concealed part of his face. Yet there was something familiar about the man, and both children instinctively stood up when he stopped in front of them. For some reason their hearts were pounding like thunder.

Then the man simply asked, "Are you ready to go?"

Arlen looked at him uncertainly. Tears stung Theodora's eyes at the sound of his voice.

"Is it you?" she whispered, so full of hope she could barely speak.

"It is I," the King smiled. He dismounted and

gathered both children in his arms. Theodora couldn't help but weep, and Arlen was speechless with pleasure.

"I've come to take you to King's Common," the King announced to explain his unexpected appearance. "I have some things to tell you as we go. This way you won't need a map or directions. I'll guide you myself. I know the way to King's Common very well, although it's been a long time since I've visited the place."

"You're taking us? I can't believe it! I just can't believe it! I hope the journey lasts forever!" Theodora danced around, beside herself with joy and excitement.

The King placed his hand softly on her head. "Let's go tell your father, Theodora. And Arlen, you'd best let your Granma know where you're going so she won't worry."

Arlen started to run, then turned back and shouted, "When will we be back?"

The King shook his head. "Just let her know that you'll be back when you've completed the task. Not a minute longer, and not a moment sooner."

"What will I need to bring?"

"You won't need a thing but the clothes you're wearing. I'll take care of the rest. Meet us at the Brighton farm, Arlen. We'll be waiting for you there."

Arlen raced like the wind toward Granma's cottage. Then the King lifted Theodora onto his own horse and sat behind her as they rode to see Burke Brighton.

Theodora's face ached with smiles as she felt the King's strong arms around her. Dreams softened her brown eyes as she imagined the wonderful days to come when she and Arlen would be traveling with the King himself.

The new adventure was beginning at last! And as for Theodora, she had never felt happier in her life.

3

The Weaver's House

BURKE BRIGHTON solemnly shook
the King's hand, patted Arlen's shoulder, and tenderly
kissed his daughter Theodora good-bye. Then, as the
three wayfarers waved farewell and disappeared behind a
hill, he wiped tears from his face. The King had caused
him to understand that Arlen and Theodora's journey
would not be an easy one.

Arlen and Theodora, however, felt nothing but

excitement to be on their way. Once again Theodora was seated in front of the King, and Arlen had the second horse all to himself.

"When we get close to King's Common," the King informed the children, "I'll leave both horses to you."

"You won't be going in with us?" Theodora was already dreading their farewell.

"No, I won't. As a matter of fact, I can't. As you'll discover, your job in King's Common will go far more easily if I am not with you."

"Why? If the people there are special heirs of your kingdom, why wouldn't you be the best one to take the book?"

"You'll see, Theodora. You'll see."

They were soon riding along Castle Street, the main road that ran through the heart of Place-Beneath-the-Castle. Its cobblestones led them past the shops and the post office and the inn called "The King's Warrior." Then the highway widened, and they found themselves crossing the Seabound River on a stone bridge. Just beyond lay the Ancient Forest.

All her life, Theodora had heard terrifying stories about the forest—about dangerous creatures that snatched travelers from their horses, about deadly attacks and dreadful disappearances. But as is often the case with such tales, no one really *knew* anyone who had vanished. Such disasters always happened to strangers, or to friends of friends of friends.

And Theodora was sure there could be no safer way to enter the Ancient Forest than with the King. He seemed thoroughly unconcerned, although ever-thickening woods threatened to block the sun out completely, while the cheery sound of the Seabound River behind them grew fainter in their ears.

"How far is it to King's Common?" Arlen asked, realizing he had no idea what lay beyond the river bridge. "Are there other villages and towns along the way?"

"It's about a three-day journey, Arlen. We'll stay in an inn tonight. Tomorrow we'll visit a friend."

Arlen wasn't entirely satisfied with the lack of details in the King's answer, but he thought better of asking for more. Meanwhile, it was impossible not to notice the sinister twisted branches overhead and the deepening darkness of the woods.

Theodora could no longer restrain herself. "King, I'm not worried or anything like that. But you know, I've heard some really frightening stories about this forest."

"Yes, I'm sure you have. But I think you'd find, even if I weren't here, that it's not quite so bad as you've heard."

"You mean there's nothing to fear?"

"No, I don't mean that at all. There is much to fear. But being afraid is usually far more terrible than facing real danger."

"Well I'm glad you're here, anyway!"

"Even if I weren't, you would only have to speak to me, and I'd send help to you." The King smiled, but Theodora shivered, thankful for his strong arms between her and the gathering gloom of the forest.

An hour or so later, Arlen said, "You know, I'm sorry to tell you this, but I'm starting to get hungry. I didn't think to bring a lunch."

"I told you not to bring a lunch, remember?" The King looked rather pleased. "I was waiting for you to ask, because I've brought along a meal prepared especially for you."

Theodora wondered why she hadn't mentioned the subject of food before. She was very hungry, indeed.

The King wasted no time taking the matter in hand. Even the road itself seemed to cooperate. The dense growth above them thinned. Sunlight streamed across the roadway. A little clearing opened up on the left, and the King steered his horse toward it. Arlen followed.

While the beasts grazed and drank from a small spring, Arlen and Theodora shared a delightful meal provided by the King. They hungrily devoured an assortment of new and delicious foods. The exotic fruits reminded Theodora of a feast they'd once enjoyed at the castle, served by beautiful, dark-eyed men and women from a distant land.

To the children's immense relief, not a threatening sound nor a discomforting creature made itself known throughout the course of the day. Once twilight fell, they could hear eerie cries somewhere behind them. But they seemed far away and, after all, the King himself was their companion.

It was nearly dark as they approached a torchlit inn, set amidst meadows along the west side of the road. "The Royal Woods," read a sign above the entrance. At the sight of it, the children dismounted, more than happy to stretch their aching legs.

The innkeeper, a red-faced man with a nervous manner, was polite enough, but his eyes never seemed to stop darting around the room. It was his lovely wife who cared for the three guests. And she did it with a radiant smile.

"Thank you so much," Theodora responded gratefully as the woman showed them to their room, handed them their towels, and told them dinner would be ready momentarily.

"To love is to serve," the woman whispered, glancing over her shoulder to see if her husband might be listening.

The dinner the woman prepared was simple — vegetables, bread, and a cup of warm broth. Yet she served it with such courtesy that it seemed far more elegant than it really was.

"Forgive me for asking, sir," she said quietly to the King, "but you seem to be someone I've known before."

"I've stayed at your inn several times in the past," he replied gently.

The woman looked around, satisfying herself that her husband was involved in a loud conversation across the room.

"Do...do you know the King?" Tense with longing, and with the risk that she might be saying the wrong thing to the wrong person, she took the chance anyway.

The children stared at their companion. How would he respond?

"Yes, dear lady, I know him well. And I want you to know something. When you serve your guests so graciously and kindly, you are truly serving the King."

Tears filled the woman's eyes. "I know he's real," she whispered. "I *know* he is!"

"Of course he's real," answered the real King. "And he sees, and he knows, and he understands."

She nodded, wiping unexpected tears from her eyes with her apron. "Your words have lifted my heart," she said. "I'd best go now and take care of the others." She walked away, glancing back at the travelers with hope shining in her eyes.

"Why didn't you tell her?" Theodora asked quietly.

"It's not yet time for her to meet me. Everything happens at the right moment when I'm involved, Theodora. Never too soon, and never too late."

Next morning the three rode away from the inn. A pale winter sun warmed their faces, and an occasional bird called out from nearby bushes. From time to time, the rushing sound of a stream or waterfall filled the morning air.

"We're going to visit a very special friend of mine," the King told the children as they trotted along. "Although the clothes you're wearing are perfectly nice for Place-Beneath-the-Castle, they won't be at all appropriate in the other villages. My friend, the weaver, will outfit you in special clothing more suitable for your journey."

Day passed into afternoon, and the countryside began to change. Large boulders lined the roadside, and stones littered the path. Pine trees appeared here and there, first on the horizon and then in small clusters beside the road. Soon whole stretches of evergreen woods pointed their graceful silhouettes skyward. Formations of clouds blew across the sky, often fogging the way for a moment. They were unusual clouds, and the children could feel them softly caressing their faces as they blew past. Carried by the breeze, the clouds lifted their hair with gentle fingers but left no trace of moisture behind.

By sunset the King, Theodora, and Arlen found themselves approaching a large cottage set in a spacious clearing. Smoke poured from three stone chimneys that stood out starkly against the chilly sky. Strange-looking nets festooned the windows. "Here we are," the King announced.

A lean, tall man appeared in the doorway. His face

lit up when he saw them. "Oh, Your Majesty, you are most welcome! I had a feeling you were coming! Please take your friends inside, and I'll be right with you." As they dismounted, he hurried out to take the reins and lead the horses toward the nearby stable.

Entering the cottage, they discovered a very unusual and busy-looking place. Spinning wheels and looms filled the room, along with mounds of varicolored threads and yarns and bolts of finely woven fabric. A fire crackled on a nearby hearth, and soon the lean man reappeared, bearing a tray, four cups, and a flask of fragrant juice.

"Mr. Weatherworth, I would like you to meet Arlen and Theodora. They are on their way to do some special tasks for me, and before they're finished, they'll need to visit a number of different villages, towns, and cities."

Theodora's eyes widened and she shot a glance at Arlen. They boy shrugged and raised his eyebrows in response. The children only knew of two destinations so far, and the King's words caused excitement to ripple through them.

"They will need garments that are acceptable anywhere they go," the King continued. "They will also require various provisions from time to time, so please sew your special pockets in place. And, by the way, I must inform you that their first visit will be at King's Common."

"No! King's Common, of all places! Now you've really given me a challenge, if you don't mind my saying so."

"I have no doubt but that you'll do very well, indeed." The King and Mr. Weatherworth laughed heartily at something they both seemed to understand very well.

"Your Majesty..." Theodora looked at Arlen, then at the King. "Why are you laughing so hard? What is so funny about King's Common?"

"Oh, child, you'll soon see. The people in King's Common have come to believe that the colors they wear show how well they know me."

"Colors?" cried Theodora. "What do colors have to do with you?"

"Nothing whatsoever, child. But over the years, these people's garments have become very important to them, and they attach great importance to wearing certain shades and hues."

"I don't understand at all." Arlen was frowning with bewilderment.

"You'll understand better once you've been there, Arlen. The people of King's Common are very confused. They think they know me, but they only know *about* me. And what they know about me isn't really true anyway. That's why I want you to take my book there. I'm hoping that some of them will actually know me by the time you leave."

Mr. Weatherworth cleared his throat politely. "So my assignment is to create garments for these two children that blend in with the various shadings around them. That's quite a task, sir!"

"Yes, Mr. Weatherworth, it *is* quite a task. Especially when you consider the fact that Arlen and Theodora are going to Mansfield once they've been to King's Common."

"Mansfield? The village of rags...Now you've really complicated things, Your Majesty! What am I to do?" The perplexed weaver stood up, walked to a window, and examined the large net which was suspended from the windowsill. He surveyed the sky, then reached inside the net with his hand.

"I'll need the finest clouds for this wardrobe," he murmured to himself, "the very finest clouds." He walked on thoughtfully from one window to the next, checking the other nets.

"He collects the clouds that blow through this part of the countryside, spins them on his wheels, and weaves marvelous, magical fabrics from their threads," explained the King. "You have noticed the exceptional clouds in this region, have you not?"

"They seem to be dry, sir," said Arlen, "and very dense."

"Yes, and they contain an amazing substance which produces fabrics that are both warm and cool, sturdy and fine, simple and beautiful."

"What about the pockets you mentioned?"

"When you have a need, be it food or drink, wisdom or wit, help or hindrance—whatever you require, you will find it by putting your hands in your pockets. You'll have to ask me first, though, or your pockets will remain quite empty!"

"You *know* what we need, sir. Why wait for us to ask?"

"Because I want you to talk to me, Theodora. Otherwise you'll be more fond of your pockets than you are of your King!"

"Never!" Theodora threw her arms around his neck and kissed him soundly on the cheek. By then Arlen was walking around the room, studying looms, examining spinning wheels, and touching various mounds of fabric, yarn, and thread.

Not many hours thereafter, each child was tucked into a clean bed beneath blankets that gleamed with light. At first neither Arlen nor Theodora thought they'd ever get to sleep, so noisy was the clatter and whir of the weaver's craft in the next room. Late into the night, they could hear Mr. Weatherworth talking to the King. But try as they might, they couldn't understand a single word.

At last they grew drowsy. Even in the darkness, a soft glow radiated from their warm blankets. And as they slept, they dreamed of nothing but the King, the castle, and the glorious book they carried with them. Their dreams were filled with joy and hope and love. How sorry they were to awaken! But for the smell of freshly baked bread that drifted in the morning air, they would have been most satisfied to stay in their beds.

After they had enjoyed a filling breakfast of hot buttered rolls and berry juice, the weaver triumphantly appeared, bearing two neatly folded piles of clothing. To Theodora he gave a long, graceful dress and a cape with a peaked hood. To Arlen he offered trousers, a shirt, and a cloak.

"Change into them now, children. I want to see how they fit."

Never in her life had Theodora so admired a dress. What color was it? At one moment, as she stood in a shadow, it shimmered with the hue of wood violets. Yet when she stepped toward the window, the rich blue of the sky seemed to spill across her skirt and sleeves.

Arlen, too, looked exceptionally handsome in his own new garments. Both children felt suddenly shy as they displayed their new clothing to the King and the weaver.

"Very good..." said the King, smiling in approval.

"Very good, if I do say so myself," repeated the weaver. "Fine bunch of clouds that blew in yesterday afternoon. Finest I've seen in years!"

The King and the weaver chuckled together. And the children, dressed in their cloud-spun attire, smiled at each other and searched for the pockets in their capes.

"They'll be empty, of course," said the weaver,

watching them with proud delight. "But then, when you're in the King's care, empty pockets simply mean that you already have everything you need!"

4

Shades of Purple

WITH MR. WEATHERWORTH'S cottage behind them, the children saw no more of the curious clouds they had encountered the day before. Now, as the sun climbed higher, they noticed more changes in their surroundings. A biting wind nipped at their hands and faces as they ascended higher and higher into a range of mountains, and soon they found themselves at the crest of a ridge.

Both Arlen and Theodora gasped in surprise as they

surveyed the view on the other side. Spread before them like a colorful quilt lay a broad valley. And from their lofty vantage point they could see several villages whose cottages and shops were bordered by fields and forests.

"There," said the King, pointing to his left. "You see the village with three tall buildings in the middle? That's King's Common."

Arlen's eyes squinted as he studied their destination. A single main street in the village seemed to lead toward the three tall structures, each of which faced the same enormous grassy field.

"That's where the town gets its name, Arlen, from that large, grassy common. Many, many years ago, I used to visit the villagers. All of them would gather there for a day's festival, to sing for me and to listen to whatever I had to say.

"In those days, many of the people really loved me." Sorrow deepened the King's voice as he continued. "And like you, Arlen, they wrote down many of my words. But once I stopped visiting King's Common, everything changed. Little by little, the villagers became more concerned with the words they had written down than they were with me. They forgot who I was and what I was like."

"So that's why they need to see your book!" Theodora was thrilled that the King's Common villagers might love their ruler again. And surely they would, once they'd seen the pages of *Tales of the King* come to life before their eyes.

"It won't be easy, Theodora. They've come to some rather strange conclusions about me by now. And they aren't going to want to change their minds."

"But once they've seen the book..."

"Theodora, the book will only come to life for those who really *want* to know me. And some of them would rather know about me than know me." The King sighed and shook his head wearily.

"No, I'll take you to the village gate, children. But there I must leave you."

Theodora was trying very hard not to cry as they approached an ornate tower just outside King's Common. She remembered the proud man in her dream. She imagined herself facing the villagers without the King. And all at once, she wanted to run back to her cottage and her family and to forget the whole assignment!

"Theodora." The King dismounted and lifted her down into his arms. His voice was soft but commanding. "It's not a good idea to begin a task for me and then turn back. Sometimes I ask you to do hard things, and I don't want to be disappointed in you because you weren't willing to try. I chose you and Arlen for this job because, with my help, you are the two very best people in all the kingdom to do it!"

"But when will we see you again?" Theodora was feeling very heartsick indeed.

"Just when you need me most. And remember, even when you don't see me, I'll be able to see you. So, in that sense, I will always be with you. Now, before I go, let's eat together."

They sat down beneath a tree and shared a final meal. The King gave them more of the delectable food they'd so enjoyed before. This time, however, he offered each of them a sip from a tiny bottle with a silver cap. They had tasted a similar bottle's contents once before, just as they had begun another challenging journey. Now, as then, it lifted their spirits, and their sadness vanished into the brisk winter air.

The King embraced the children, holding each child firmly to his chest. "It's time for you to go. Take the book, ask for a man named Lord Lilac, and...oh, yes! Don't forget your pockets!"

And so it was that, all too soon, Arlen and Theodora were bidding the King good-bye and walking up to the big gate that marked the village entrance. Place-Beneath-the-Castle had no such security measures, and they weren't quite sure what to do. All at once a guard appeared. He had a puffy face, and behind thick spectacles his eyes looked dimly confused. But he was regally garbed in a bright purple uniform, and he wore a golden crown set with a dull, red jewel.

Theodora suddenly noticed that Arlen's cloak and trousers were nearly as purple as the guard's attire. Just minutes before they had reflected only the green of the surrounding trees and grass. She glanced at her skirt. It gleamed with purple light.

"Where are you going?"

"Into King's Common," Arlen replied confidently.

"And what is your business there?"

"We've got a book..." Theodora began.

"Oh, you're with the book dealers. I see, I see..." The guard studied them carefully. They were wearing purple, all right. And they were involved in books, which were very important items in the village. But they were only children. And they had no crowns.

Befuddled for a moment, he finally asked, "With which shade of purple do you identify yourselves?"

"What do you mean? Can't you see what we're wearing?" Arlen's quick response stopped that line of questioning.

"Is anyone expecting you?"

Arlen and Theodora looked at each other, and the girl nervously put her hand in her pocket. "Lord Lilac!" she blurted out, remembering the King's instructions. "We need to see Lord Lilac!"

"Mmmm...yes. Lord Lilac. He's our mayor, you know." The guard thumbed through a leatherbound directory of some sort. "Mmmm...yes, here it is. Yes. Wisdom Lane, number 4. Turn left just past the Common."

Much relieved, the children set out toward the heart

of the village. At first nothing seemed exceptional about the place. People came and went, nodding politely as they passed. But soon Arlen and Theodora realized that everyone was dressed in purple in one of three shades—light, medium, or dark. And every person wore a crown. Some crowns were small, with no jewels. Others were larger and more lavish.

Strangely, however, none of the jewels in the crowns or on the villagers' clothing glittered or sparkled, not even in the sunlight. Like those in Theodora's dream, they looked cheap and vaguely artificial. But the men, women, and children of King's Common carried themselves with such pride that their gaudy decorations were soon forgotten.

Arlen and Theodora continued their walk through the village. As they rounded a bend in the road, they came upon an immense lawn. "The Common!" Arlen exclaimed. And there, bordering it on three sides, stood the trio of massive structures they had seen hours before from the crest of the mountains.

Each building was monumental in size. The first was constructed almost entirely of glass, and inset with violet-hued gemstones. Its many windows reflected the sunlight, and its portals ascended loftily above the children's heads. Over its glass doors, a carefully painted sign read,

THE KING KNOWS

(Meetings on Wednesdays)

Across the green field, another elaborate structure was put together entirely of stones, each one cut into beautiful, decorative shapes. It was every bit as tall as its glass neighbor. The mortar that held the stones in place was of a purplish hue, as were the panes in its round windows. A signboard above its wooden doors said,

THE KING FEELS

(Meetings on Fridays)

To their left, a third building carved of fine wood towered mightily over the common. The intricately decorated moldings around its windows and doors were painted royal purple, and its sign proclaimed,

THE KING UNDERSTANDS

(Meetings Daily, Dawn and Dusk)

Arlen and Theodora were speechless. Such grand and glorious architecture, all dedicated to their beloved King! They gazed at the buildings, their eyes trying to absorb all the magnificent details. With such monuments built in his honor, why was the King unhappy about this village?

"I don't understand this at all. Do you, Arlen?" Theodora often expected her clever friend to figure out the things that puzzled her. But this time he was as mystified as she was. He simply shook his head and murmured, "I guess we'd better find Lord Lilac now."

Without much difficulty, the children located Wisdom Lane, number 4, and tapped on the door. It swung open, and who should be standing there but the man in Theodora's dream! She caught her breath in wonder. It was the same portly man, to be sure. But this time he was, in fact, wearing a crown—a thick gold band set with multicolored stones and circling his forehead.

"What can I do for you children?" For some reason, the man seemed to be scrutinizing their clothes and their heads.

"We were sent by the King to find you, sir."

Lord Lilac's face flushed. "Pardon me? You were sent by whom?"

"By the King, sir. He told us to find you."

The man looked up and down the street and from side to side, as if he were afraid someone might be listening. Rather reluctantly, he invited the children inside.

"I see that you value books, sir!" Arlen's hand swept through the air, indicating his admiration for the mayor's expansive library.

"Yes, we need to read all we can about our King, don't we? But children, where are your crowns?"

Theodora was undaunted in her enthusiasm. "We have no crowns, sir. But we've brought something better—a wonderful book about the King. This is surely the best book of all!"

The man visibly stiffened. "Well, of course, the quality of your book will be decided at the meetingplace. Who is the author, may I ask?"

"Why the King himself, sir. He gave it to us at his castle and told us to take it around the kingdom."

Theodora reverently placed the golden book in Lord Lilac's hands. He opened it uncertainly. But it was soon evident, judging by the expression on his face, that no words were coming to life for him.

"It looks like rather heavy reading to me," he commented coldly. "But the other leaders will take a look at it. You're fortunate, because we meet tonight. It's Wednesday. Those of us who believe the King knows meet on Wednesday."

Not long thereafter, the children found themselves inside the tall, glass building, which was rapidly filling up with villagers of all ages.

"Look, Arlen. These people all wear the medium purple shade, the sort of lilac color," Theodora commented.

Arlen nodded, his arms folded solidly across his chest. The boy wasn't the least bit pleased at having their mission held in question.

At last the meeting started. First a woman sang a

mournful song entitled, "Oh, So Few Have Known the King Who Knows."

After her solo, a number of different people quoted confusing words from several large books. At long last, the main speaker closed his lengthy message with the phrase, "The King knows." Everyone murmured the words back to him, adding, "And we know him best. We are the true heirs." Finally they all filed outside.

On the steps of the edifice, Lord Lilac introduced the children to the speaker, an elderly man with a most elaborate crown. "They say they've brought a book from the King."

The old man shook his head sadly. "Not likely. Not likely at all. But let's have a look."

Arlen handed him the golden volume. He opened it and seemed to be trying to comprehend its words. They followed him back inside, where he sat down and pored over the book for several minutes.

"Now, now," he concluded, "we know better, don't we? Another fraud, I fear. I do think, however, that our neighbors who believe the King feels might be interested. They have an emotional need to discover new things, you see." The old man snickered. "Take it to their Friday meeting."

Arlen and Theodora were soon left to themselves in the middle of the village common, all alone in the moonlight. "A fraud! How dare they, Arlen? What are we going to do?"

"Well, the 'King Understands' sign says there are daily meetings in that building. We'll go there tomorrow and go to the other meeting on Friday."

"But where will we sleep? And what are we going to eat?" Tears burned in Theodora's eyes. Both children felt overwhelmed with disappointment and discouragement. "Arlen, they think we're liars. They don't believe us!"

Arlen's deep frown answered her. He shoved his hands in his pockets. Finally he spoke. "I just wish the King were here to tell us what to do..."

Across the common a door slammed. A lean young man stalked down a walkway and made his way across the grass. When he saw the boy and girl, he stopped and stared at them. Like everyone else, he was dressed in a shade of purple. But no crown graced his head, and his clothes bore no ornaments. "Who are you?" he asked abruptly.

"I'm Arlen, and this is my friend Theodora. Would you happen to know of a guest house where we could spend the night?"

"No, there's no guest house in this village. But you can stay with my mother and me. We love visitors, and we haven't had many since I lost my crown. I'm Duncan, by the way, and I was just out for a breath of air, but the walk can wait. Let me take you to Mother. I can't help but notice that you've got no crowns, either."

Striding quickly toward Duncan's cottage, Theodora's mind was flooded with questions, but she wisely limited herself to just one. "How did you lose your crown, Duncan?"

"By trying to learn more about the King," Duncan replied quietly. "I wanted so much to *know* him and not just know *about* him. But they took away my crown because I questioned some of their most dearly held beliefs."

"They?" Arlen asked. "Who are 'they'?"

"The leaders, of course," Duncan gravely replied.

"Oh, Duncan, wait till you see the book we've brought—it's from the King himself!" Theodora burst out. "You *can* know him, Duncan. Just wait till you see our book!"

"Books, books, books." Duncan shook his head dejectedly. "Considering all that's happened to me, I honestly don't know if I ever want to look at another book! To tell you the truth, I'm not even sure there really is a King, after all."

5

Of Kings and Crowns

"YOU ARE SO VERY welcome, children!" Duncan's mother, Rose, beamed at the sight of her unexpected guests. A short, plump woman, she was pinafored in purple and wore a thin circlet of gold around her head.

"Thank you so much for your hospitality, ma'am." Finishing a simple meal of fruit and cheese, Arlen rubbed his eyes as he spoke. "We are really very tired."

"Then not another word! To bed with both of you.

Any talk about your visit to King's Common can wait until tomorrow."

"What about the book?" In spite of his doubts, Duncan's curiosity had been aroused.

"Not another word, son! Let the poor darlings rest. Tomorrow will be here soon enough, and you can ask your questions then!"

Minutes later, Arlen and Theodora found themselves in a small, cozy room and tucked into two tiny beds, each with a blue-violet coverlet and an eyelet pillow. A peacefulness pervaded the house and, in spite of their disappointing day, the children drifted to sleep without a moment's restlessness.

Next morning Theodora, eager to show Duncan the book, was up, scrubbed, and dressed before Arlen opened his eyes. But Arlen soon joined her and her hosts at the breakfast table.

"So what brings you to our village?" Rose inquired politely as she served the children toast and tea.

"The King sent us here with a book. He wants us to show it to the people of the kingdom so they can know him better and love him more."

"The King, you say. And a book? May I see it?" Rose's eyes glowed softly, and her voice was unsteady.

"Of course you can!" Theodora rushed to the bedroom and gladly presented the golden book to her hostess. Rose opened it slowly, gently feeling the beautiful parchment pages with her fingertips. Then, all at once, she gasped aloud. The words had begun to spring to life right before her eyes!

"Duncan! Look!" She could hardly speak. Her son leaned over her shoulder. He wiped his eyes with his handkerchief, not trusting what he saw. In a moment, mother and son were watching the tales of the King unfold. And for the first time in their lives, they were actually getting to know the King, not just hearing about him!

How long did they look at the book? No one was ever quite sure, but eventually Rose shook her head and closed the golden cover. She touched Duncan's cheek with her hand. "We were right, son, weren't we?"

"We were, indeed, Mother. But the others will never believe it."

"Some will. We'll invite a few friends to dinner tonight, Duncan. We'll see what happens."

Arlen and Theodora were greatly relieved. At least two people in King's Common really did want to know the King!

Encouraged, Arlen told Duncan and Rose, "We need to take the book to the other meetingplaces tonight and tomorrow. They should have a chance to read it, too."

"And once they see it come to life, of course they'll believe! The whole village will be changed!" The woman bustled aimlessly about her kitchen in sheer delight.

"I wish it were true," replied Theodora. "But the

King says that unless people really *want* to believe in the first place, they won't be able to see the pages come to life. Lord Lilac thought the book was terribly boring. And the speaker at 'The King Knows' meeting said it was an absolute fraud." Theodora shuddered at the unpleasant memory of the night before.

Rose and Duncan looked at each other and shook their heads. "Well, I have to admit, that surprises me," said Rose. "In that case, I don't think you'll have much better success at the other two meetingplaces," she commented. "But I suppose you'll have to try, won't you?"

And try they did.

Thursday's "The King Understands" meeting began with all the deep-purple-clad people repeating together, "We understand that the King understands, and we understand him best."

Once the subject of the golden book was introduced, the group became violently incensed with Arlen and Theodora. The leaders accused them of representing the Six Cruel Kings and roughly escorted them out of their beautiful building.

"You are fools, at best!" snarled one of the bejeweled leaders. "And more likely than not, you are evil ambassadors! Outsiders are always trying to corrupt our community with lies. But we have the true understanding. We write the true books. And we are the true heirs!"

Friday's "The King Feels" group was less angry. That

meeting began with their pale-violet-garbed congre-
gation singing softly, "We feel that our King feels, and
that our King feels our feelings."

The children were introduced politely. And a few
faces in that crowd actually seemed to brighten at the
news of a wonderful golden book brought from the King's
castle. Unfortunately, the leaders were not so receptive.

"We have strong feelings about our King, dear little
ones, and we've written many beautiful books
ourselves—books of poetry and song. There is not one
thing about the King we haven't already felt. You are
nothing more than simple, uneducated children. We are
the true heirs to the kingdom!"

On both Thursday and Friday nights, after the
children's sound rejection at the large meetingplaces,
Rose and Duncan invited several of their friends for
dinner. Without exception, the visitors saw the pages of
the book unfold before their eyes, and all of them left
rejoicing. In an unpredicted and unexpected way, each
had met the King at last.

"Duncan," asked Arlen just before bedtime on
Friday night, "Who took away your crown? Which
group? Which meetingplace?"

"All three," Duncan replied with a bitter laugh.

"But they don't agree about anything! How could
they agree about your crown?"

Rose spoke up, her face flushed with anger. "Oh,
yes, they dispute about knowing and feeling and

understanding. But when my Duncan said the King was too big to have heirs in only one village, well, *all* the leaders were insulted and enraged. And when Duncan tried to leave King's Common to search for the King, they all agreed that he could never again wear his crown—not for the rest of his life!"

"What difference does a crown make, anyway?" Arlen thought the whole idea of crowns was absurd.

"Well, it makes quite a bit of difference, I'm sorry to say. To begin with, not having a crown means I'll never have a decent job, and I'll never be allowed to marry. And that's not to mention the insults and abuse I have to live with every day."

Arlen shook his head in disbelief. "How do you get your crowns in the first place?"

"In all three meetingplaces, the leaders place them on newborn babies' heads during a special ceremony. Later in life, jewels are added as a reward for reading books or memorizing facts or listening to stories. The jewels represent various levels of accomplishment."

"So the bigger the crown, the more you know...or feel...or understand?"

"Yes, that's it."

"But what about doing kind things for other people? Can you get jewels for that?"

"Not anymore. In the old days, good deeds were

important. But now, it's just learning all you can about the King. That's what really matters."

"Do the three groups ever meet together?" Theodora recalled hearing about the long-ago festivals when all the villagers had joyfully gathered on the Common to greet the King.

"The three groups will only agree to gather in the common for one purpose," Rose said, "and that's to judge someone who goes against the beliefs of the entire village. That's what happened to Duncan."

"And let me warn you, Arlen," Duncan said grimly. "Children or not, I think it could happen to you and Theodora, too."

He had hardly said the words when there was a knock at the door. Rose opened it, and Lord Lilac strode pompously into the humble cottage, followed by opulently crowned leaders from all three meetingplaces.

"I see you heretics like to stick together," he commented icily. No one answered him, so he unfolded a pale purple sheet of parchment and began to read from it.

"The United Board of Leaders commands that the two foreign children who call themselves Arlen and Theodora should stand trial on the Village Common Saturday night at eight. It will be decided at that time whether or not said children are representatives of the Six Cruel Kings. Said children are to bring with them the book, so-called *Tales of the King*. Should they fail to appear, their friends"—he motioned haughtily toward

Rose and Duncan—"will bear the consequences for their crimes."

The leaders accompanying Lord Lilac murmured in assent.

"We know about the secret meetings you've been having here all week. Nothing has escaped our notice!" Lord Lilac announced in conclusion, and the proud entourage marched out the door without further comment.

"You see? You see what happens?" Duncan paced around and around the room. "What's to become of us all?"

Arlen and Theodora felt shaken and sick at heart. What kind of tragedy had they brought into this friendly home? Silence hung heavily in the house for several moments.

"What if we leave the village now and don't go to the meeting?" Theodora wondered out loud.

Rose brushed her hand across the girl's long hair. "You'll have to appear at the meeting for all of our sakes. I'm sure they will force you to leave the village afterward. But before you go, we'll have some friends over for a nice farewell supper here at the house. I won't have you two leaving without proper good-byes."

Saturday night, Rose proved herself to be not only as good as her word, but courageous as well. She prepared a delicious feast, lovingly served from her humble kitchen. And she welcomed twenty guests—every person in the village who had read the book and seen its pages come to life.

After supper, Rose stood up and addressed her guests. "Perhaps you've already heard what's going to happen at eight o'clock tonight, but perhaps you haven't. Because of the book, these two precious children"—she placed a kindly hand on each child's head—"are about to be tried by the United Board of Leaders. They are accused of being liars and of representing the Six Cruel Kings."

Her guests responded in horror and disgust as Rose continued to speak.

"Naturally all of us will be affected by this trial. You can be sure that every one of us will be accused of participating in their 'crime.' But I just want Arlen and Theodora to know that we're their friends, no matter what. And I especially want to thank them for bringing the King's beautiful book to us."

"Yes, thank you so much. How can we thank you?" Everyone stood up and hugged the children. Anger and sorrow lined the faces of these villagers. Then an old man spoke.

"I think it's safe to say that all of us here believe the King hears us when we speak. Should we not, then, ask for his help?"

The room fell suddenly silent and remained so for several moments.

"Oh, King!" Theodora put her hands in her pockets,

and her soft voice spoke out clearly. "Please help us! We really need you. Arlen and I can leave the village, but these poor friends can't. They are the ones who will suffer. We've done our best with your book. Please show us what to do next!"

No one spoke. No one moved. Apart from a clock ticking in the next room, no sound could be heard. Then a voice broke through the stillness.

"You needn't be afraid." Theodora's eyes widened when she heard it, and Arlen jumped to his feet and looked around. The King himself was standing in the room with them, leaning casually against the kitchen wall as if he had been there all along. "You don't need to be afraid at all."

"Who is he?" one of the guests whispered suspiciously.

"Don't you recognize him from the book? He looks like the King to me!"

"The King? He's not dressed like a king. He's wearing riding clothes of some sort."

"Yes, I see, but I'm sure it's him."

The King spoke again, and by now everyone realized who he was. "The trial will take place, and the children will be cast out of the village. All of you will lose your crowns."

The people gasped in dread. Hadn't he just said, "Don't be afraid?" Didn't he understand the disgrace and disaster losing their crowns would cause?

The King went on. "I'm going to take Arlen and Theodora away with me tonight. The rest of you will only remain in King's Common a little longer."

"Why? Then what? What will we do?"

"There are still a few more people in this village who sincerely want to know me. Before you go, just tell them you've met me, and report everything you've seen. Once the last of them knows, I'll send my messengers to rescue you all."

"Where are we going?"

"I've planned a new life for you in a village where you won't need crowns to survive. And do be patient. You'll be there sooner than you might imagine."

The old man watched the King gravely, compassion for his fellow villagers reflected in his eyes. "Shouldn't we try to reason with the meetingplace leaders, now that we've actually seen you?"

The King shook his head emphatically. "No! There's no point to it. They've refused to believe for generations. Pride is more important to them than truth."

"What will become of them, Your Majesty?"

The King crossed his arms, smiled, and shrugged.

"They will stay. You will go. They will continue to treasure their artificial crowns. You will give yours up so you can receive real crowns in my castle. They will die honoring a King who never was. You will live honoring a King who knows...and feels...and understands."

Having finished speaking, the King turned to Arlen and Theodora. "Do you have the book?" he asked.

"It's right here," answered Arlen, tucking it carefully under his arm.

The King turned once more to the awestruck villagers. "Be patient and brave, dear friends. And remember, when you call out to me, I always hear you."

With that, they all headed for the village common. Rose's friends joined the crowd. The King stood inconspicuously next to the children. And when they stole a glance at him, they saw that he was no longer garbed in riding clothes.

Instead, he wore a robe of the richest purple velvet, flashing with diamonds. On his head was a golden, jeweled crown that gleamed like fire in the moonlight. His face was etched with authority. His posture was erect and dignified.

And neither Arlen nor Theodora could recall ever seeing their King look so very, very determined.

6

True Heirs

A CROWD QUICKLY gathered on
the grassy field, and it seemed to Arlen and Theodora
that every villager in King's Common was there. Even in
the rapidly fading twilight, they could see that the people
were divided into three distinct groups, each defined by
the shades of purple they wore and the loud songs they
sang. A deafening disharmony filled the night air, for
each group was noisily trying to outsing the others.

Leaders of the three meetingplaces sat regally on a platform facing the crowd, along with Lord Lilac.

Arlen and Theodora stood quietly next to the platform in an area where the leaders had ordered them to wait. From time to time they glanced at the King, unable to read his thoughts. The expression of grim determination upon his face kept them from speaking to him.

Once the chaotic singing had died down, Lord Lilac spoke with great pomp. "As most of you know, two children are being tried tonight. These evil brats, so-called Arlen and Theodora"—with disgust he gestured toward the two children—"came here with a book they claimed to have received from our King.

"We welcomed them warmly, of course, as is our manner. And some of us, who belong to the meetingplace of those who *know*—"

A roaring cheer from the "know" section of the crowd interrupted him. He held up his hand with a smug smile and continued, "—those who *know* recall a prophecy given generations ago stating, 'In the final days of the kingdom, two children will bring golden truth.'

"Naturally, we wanted to assure ourselves that these two were not the promised children. And we wanted our fellow meetingplaces to make their own decisions about the children, too."

A tide of angry controversy roared across the

common. The know group, the feel group, and the understand group were quarreling among themselves, debating about the prophecy. They all acknowledged that it certainly wasn't being fulfilled. They simply could not agree as to why.

Lord Lilac pounded on the podium with his fist, and after several minutes order was restored. He turned to the meetingplace leaders behind him. "Despite our *many* differences," he smiled stiffly, "are we all in agreement that these two children have *not* fulfilled the prophecy?"

The leaders nodded, mumbling "Hear, hear."

"All right," continued Lord Lilac. "What shall we do with them, then?"

The crowd shouted in unison, "Out of our village! Out of our village! Throw them out of our village!"

"Do you agree?" Lord Lilac asked the leaders.

"Hear, hear," the leaders nodded again.

"And what about their miserable friends, those who have believed their lies?"

"Away with their crowns! Away with their crowns!" screamed the angry citizens.

"Do you agree with that, too?" Lord Lilac inquired of the men behind him. "Hear, hear," they agreed yet again.

"Infidels, bring forth your crowns!"

One by one, as their names were called out, the men and women who had visited Rose and Duncan's home made their way to the front of the crowd. As they approached the leaders of the meetingplaces, they took off their crowns and handed them over.

"Disgraced! Disgraced!" chanted the angry crowd.

"Disgraced, indeed," declared Lord Lilac, watching the humiliated villagers, bare of head and broken of heart, trudge away into the night.

Theodora wiped her eyes and Arlen struggled with unforgiving thoughts as they saw their new friends' shameful treatment. But then something happened that neither of them had anticipated. The King himself strode onto the platform, his steps firm and his head high.

Lord Lilac stepped backward and froze in place. A hush fell upon the vast audience of villagers. Who was this splendid stranger? What shade was his purple robe? Why were his jewels so exceptionally bright?

"There is yet another prophecy"—the King's voice cut through the night air, cold as a blade of steel—"that you have all forgotten: 'The true heirs to the kingdom will receive their crowns from the King himself.'

"*You* are the impostors, all of you who treasure false jewels and guard your foolish village crowns.

"*You* are the liars, all of you who claim to be heirs of the kingdom.

"*You* are the representatives of the Six Cruel Kings who refuse to love.

"*You* most surely are *not* the King's true or special

heirs. In fact, I can tell you with absolute certainty that you would not recognize your King even if you saw him with your own eyes!"

The King stalked away from the King's Common platform. He walked resolutely down the two wooden steps. Then he took Theodora and Arlen by the hand and led them through the dumbstruck crowd, down the main street of the village, and out through the unguarded gate.

By the time the three reached the horses, patiently grazing in a nearby field, the King was wearing his riding clothes again and a smile had returned to his face.

"You did well, children. Very well. I'm proud of you both!"

"But we never convinced the leaders about the book, Your Majesty." Theodora felt like a failure. "No matter what we said or how strongly we argued, we couldn't make them believe us."

The King laughed. "Arguments are of little use with such people, Theodora. And you did your best. That's all you can ever do."

Arlen looked down at the beautiful, golden book he still carried in his hands. He had suddenly become aware that he and Theodora had only accomplished half of their assignment.

"Well, then, sir. How do we get from here to Mansfield?"

"And what's going to happen to us there?"

Theodora felt drained and disheartened. Only the King's presence gave her courage, and she clung to his hand.

"First we'll rest in a cottage not far from here. Some of my messengers have prepared it for us. Then, tomorrow, I'll take you to the outskirts of Mansfield."

* * * * *

It would have taken them less than an hour to ride to the cottage had a storm not slowed them down considerably. Blowing snow driven by a brutal wind stung their cheeks and made their hands and faces ache. How relieved they were, by the end of the journey, to find themselves in a cozy room, cheered by a crackling fireplace. A simple meal awaited them. Soon hearty soup, hot bread, milk, and nutcakes filled Arlen and Theodora with warmth and lifted their spirits.

The King began to discuss their next destination. "Mansfield is larger than a village. It's actually more the size of a township or even a small city. And it is a place of great tragedy, children." The King poked at the fire with a stick as he spoke.

"The harm done in King's Common is accomplished with personal disgrace and humiliation. But in Mansfield, it's different. The people who love me there are physically mistreated. They are some of my most faithful friends. And no one has suffered more than they."

Theodora's stomach tightened. "Will we be mistreated, too?"

"You're frightened again, aren't you?" The King studied the little girl carefully, his face catching the flickering shadows of the fire. "You will not be severely hurt, but you will share in the suffering of my friends. You will experience their pain, just as they will be encouraged by you and by my book."

"I hope we can make them feel better! The woman in my dream was so miserable." Arlen could still see her tired eyes and her thin neck and arms.

"There is something else to watch out for in Mansfield, Arlen. Something besides misery. There are creatures there who torment my friends."

"Creatures? Like the rainbow beings?"

The King smiled. "Nothing so big and bold as that, I'm afraid. These are small, unseen creatures called 'whisperers.' They are the handiwork of the Six Cruel Kings, who bred them, trained them, and then made them invisible. Whisperers are forever breathing lies into the ears of my people. The result is that my friends in Mansfield trust me, but they do not trust each other. There is a terrible division among them. Only those in the dungeon are united, because they have so little left to lose."

"What can we do about the whisperers? Will they lie to us, too?"

"If you put your hands into your pockets, you'll be

able to see them, even without asking me. Just order them to leave, and use my name, and they'll run away from you."

"Will they hurt us?"

"Not unless you forget how dangerous they can be."

That night, with icy snow tinkling against the windows, the children slept warm under cloud-woven blankets that only Mr. Weatherworth could have created. And what dreams they had—of the King's magnificent castle, of singing and laughing with beloved friends they'd yet to meet; of magical ships and moonlit flights, and faraway lands where the King still ate and drank and danced with his people.

When they awoke, they were surging with energy, fit and ready for the days to come. Theodora pulled open the lace curtains on the cottage windows, and rays of golden light streaked across the room. The storm was over, and the snowy world outside the cottage sparkled brilliantly in the sun. There was very little to do on such a lovely morning but be happy.

Had Theodora and Arlen been able to see the events that would transpire in the next few days, perhaps they would have been less eager for their visit to Mansfield to begin. But right then, in the King's presence, nothing seemed too difficult. They felt sure that he would take care of any challenges that might befall.

Once breakfast was over, the floor swept, and the

dishes done, the King said, "It's time we resumed our journey. I want you to arrive in Mansfield well before dark, for curfew begins after sundown, and you won't be at all safe after that."

"What's a curfew?" Theodora whispered to Arlen.

"A law that tells people what time they have to go inside their houses and stay there." Arlen's tutor in the City of Bells had taught him well. And just then, the King began a lesson of his own.

"The ruler of Mansfield is an evil, cruel man called Prince Newcastle. The town was once known as Kingsfield. Newcastle was sent there by the Six Cruel Kings to transform it into a headquarters for their rebellion. The Six sent the first whisperers into the town along with the Prince.

"At the outset, Prince Newcastle was very cooperative with the Six Cruel Kings and did everything just as they requested. But once he got a taste of power, he began to build a corrupt empire of his own.

"The Six have never really opposed him, since evil is evil, and they are always glad to see my people suffer. But they have lost control over him now, and he has become an independent tyrant. Consequently, without the support of the Six, the townspeople are terribly poor and hungry. Only the Prince, his advisers, and his warriors live in luxury.

"Prince Newcastle hates nothing more than me. He has removed my name from everything in the town. And he cruelly enjoys torturing the townspeople who know and love me. His dungeon is filled with my friends."

The three mounted their horses and rode westward. As they descended a little further into the valley, they left the snow behind, and the air became warmer. There were few distractions along the way, and the King had little more to say.

"I hope our clothes will look all right in Mansfield," Theodora glanced down at her skirt, which shimmered with sunlit clouds and blue skies.

"Yes," Arlen nodded. "I've been thinking about that. I hope we aren't so well dressed that the people feel bad about their own poor rags. I've never seen such rags as in my dream..."

"The weaver has done well, children. Once you are surrounded with rags, you will appear to be in rags, too. And it must be so. In order to take my messages around the kingdom, you must always learn to fit in with the people you're visiting. Otherwise they will feel uncomfortable, and they won't listen to a thing you have to say to them."

Theodora understood perfectly. "It's true. In King's Common, the weaver's cloth was so carefully colored that no one was ever quite sure which shade of purple we were wearing."

"Clever man, Mr. Weatherworth." The King chuckled softly to himself. "And by the way, you won't be seeing any crowns in Mansfield."

"What about the crown I saw in my dream?" Arlen still remembered its shimmering lacework with awe.

"Like all my true heirs, Mara will receive her crown someday when she comes to my castle. She just doesn't *know* about it yet."

On the horizon, a tall, gray wall rose ominously before them, topped by a thorny hedge. Every few feet a turret rose grimly above the edifice. And in each turret, an armed man stood at attention, his eyes scanning the countryside below.

"Welcome to Mansfield, children." The King's eyes filled with tears as he spoke.

"How will we ever get in?"

"My messengers will take you in, Theodora. Otherwise you'd never get past the wall."

Arlen looked directly at the King. "And how will we get out, sir?"

Sadness shadowed the King's face as he fixed his eyes on them.

"I will precede you, and I will follow you. Good-bye, children. Remember your pockets. Watch out for the whisperers. And give my love to my people."

7

An Unlawful Assembly

CLOUDS SWIRLED ABOVE their
heads, and the icy wind nearly took their breath away.
When they looked up, they saw only the sun. When they
looked down, they saw a miniature township, surrounded
by a forbidding gray wall. When they looked at each
other, Arlen and Theodora found that they were firmly
tucked under the strong arms of a rainbow messenger,
whose shimmering form flew swiftly across the afternoon
sky.

The next thing they knew, the two children were in a dingy room furnished with a table, a narrow bed, and a broken chair. They were standing in front of a woman whose face had grown pale with alarm at the sight of two small, uninvited visitors.

It's her! The woman from my dream! Arlen thought to himself, but he didn't dare speak the words.

"Where did you come from?" The ragged woman looked wildly around the room and whispered hoarsely. "And where did the food come from?"

The children followed her gaze to a table, which was set for three people. Glasses of milk and plates of bread, cheese, and fruit waited to be eaten.

"We haven't had fruit here for more than ten years. And milk? I can't even remember milk!" The woman was talking to herself, not to the children, so great was her amazement.

Theodora squeezed the woman's thin hand in hers. "Ma'am, please forgive us for coming to your home uninvited. But the King sent us. One of his messengers brought us here, and..."

"Shhh, not so loud!" The woman frantically closed her curtains. "Speak softly, child! There is always someone listening."

Arlen picked up the story from Theodora, who was feeling a bit embarrassed. "We were sent to bring this book to you. That's why we're here—to encourage all the

King's friends by showing them this book and by giving them a message of his love."

The woman gazed at the book, then at the table, then at the children's earnest faces. "Forgive me. My name is Mara, and I have been terribly rude to you. The King has surely sent you, or you could never have come. And this food...oh, we are always so very hungry. Do come and eat with me, and tell me your names."

Still she whispered, but the panic in her face was fading into a sort of tense wariness. "Arlen? Theodora? I'm so very pleased to meet two children of the King. Very pleased, indeed."

Arlen and Theodora noticed that Mara ate her portion of the meal very quickly; in fact, she had nearly finished when they had scarcely begun. They gave her some of their own food, and she rapidly devoured that, too.

"What about the book you've brought? What is it?"

"It's a book about the King, Mara. The pages come to life when people who know him read it."

"Here it is," said Arlen, and he placed it in Mara's hands. She opened it and caught her breath. "Oh, our beloved King! It's so good to see his lovely face again! He's been here to visit us, you know."

She began to cry and to turn the pages ever so slowly, as if not wanting to rush a visit with a dear and long-missed friend.

"Oh, children, how can I thank you for bringing this to me? It is so precious..."

"You needn't thank us, Mara," Arlen replied, "But you could help us find some of the King's other friends, so they can see it too."

Mara looked at Arlen uncertainly. Her mind seemed to be confused somehow, and her expression passed from friendly to mistrustful. "How do I know you won't betray me?" she asked harshly.

The children's thoughts were exactly the same. *What on earth changed her attitude so suddenly? It's as if someone were telling her not to trust us...a whisperer!*

Theodora glanced at Arlen. He nodded. They both put their hands in their pockets. And, sure enough, on Mara's shoulder, they saw an ugly, rodent-like creature that was muttering something in her ear.

"They'll get you in trouble with Prince Newcastle," they heard it say. "That's why they're here. They were sent to get you arrested and thrown in jail."

"Mara!" Arlen spoke firmly and abruptly. "There's something else the King wanted us to tell you."

She looked up at him uncertainly, struck by the authority in his young voice. "What's that?"

"You cannot see it, but on your shoulder is a small, ugly creature who is whispering lies into your ear. The King calls these creatures whisperers."

Mara's face was a mask of bewilderment. "There's

nothing on my shoulder, Arlen. I can't feel a thing." Her hand moved in the direction of the creature, and it backed away.

"Get away from her!" Theodora cried out. "The King says for you to get away!" The little rodent scurried across the room and vanished.

"It's gone." Arlen smiled, glad to see that the little beasts really were afraid of the King's name.

"Are you two mad?" Mara put her forehead in her hand and shook her head. "Whisperers?"

"Mara, do the people in Mansfield who love the King mistrust each other?"

"Everyone in Mansfield mistrusts everyone else, Theodora. Prince Newcastle has spies everywhere. Every family has informers—brothers and sisters, mothers and fathers. The little gatherings of friends who love the King are always being broken up by arrests, and the deception always comes from within the group. It has to! How else would the prince's warriors know?"

"They know because of the whisperers. That's what you need to understand. The whisperers are spies! The King's friends would never deceive each other."

"Well, the prince's friends certainly would! No one knows who is loyal to whom. We have a very difficult life here, children. And your talk of whisperers confuses me. Still, I do believe that the King sent you. Look at your arrival—the food, the book. Who else but the King could do such things?"

"Give some thought to what we've told you, Mara. But meanwhile, how can we reach the King's other friends? Surely you know who they are!"

"I know, all right. But I know they'd never trust me again if I sent you to them. They'd never trust you, either."

"They'll trust us once they see the book." Arlen was beginning to feel a little frustrated. Why was this so complicated?

"They'll never see the book if they won't let you into their homes. I wouldn't have let you in myself if you hadn't materialized right in the middle of my house!"

"Couldn't you invite some of the King's friends to your home? Wouldn't they talk to us here?" Theodora gratefully recalled Rose's gracious dinner parties, events which had so simplified the children's mission to King's Common.

"Invite them here? I'd never invite anyone here! I live alone, and I prefer to be alone. I leave my house only to search for food."

Arlen and Theodora weren't at all sure what to do or what to say. Then Arlen whispered something to himself and slowly put his hand in his pocket. His face suddenly lit up.

"Do you know a man named Mr. Freemaster?" he asked.

The question caught Mara off guard. "Why yes, as a matter of fact I do. Freemaster lives on the next street, fifth house on the right, and he is a friend of the King. That's a good idea, dear. Go see him. Maybe he can help you."

Mara was more than happy for the children to leave. Even though she had been deeply touched by the golden book, she was uncomfortable with their presence. Like many of the King's friends in Mansfield, fear had isolated her so long that she was unable to enjoy the company of others, even though they brought gifts from the King himself.

After waving good-bye to Mara, the children hurried along the filthy street, stepping high over rubbish and decaying leaves. They turned right, then left, and knocked on the door of the fifth house.

Locks clicked inside, and the door opened just far enough to allow someone to peek through. "Who are you?" whispered a man's voice.

"We're friends of the King."

There was a prolonged delay. The man seemed to be considering his next move. "Are you Mr. Freemaster?" Arlen whispered.

No answer. Again, a long wait. Finally, the door opened a little wider. The children saw a gaunt, bespectacled man dressed in tattered trousers and a patched tunic. "Come in," he said quietly.

Once inside, the children looked around at another squalid room, one even more sparsely furnished than

Mara's. This time the table was empty, and there was no bed, only a rough blanket folded beneath a stained pillow.

"You're probably spies," Mr. Freemaster said with resignation in his voice. "But if you say you know the King, I can't very well leave you standing outside, can I?"

"We were sent by the King to bring this book to Mansfield, sir." Arlen handed him the book. Freemaster sat down at the table and held the golden cover in his hands. He turned the pages toward a window and adjusted his spectacles. Then he caught his breath.

"Why it's the King, all right! Where did you get this book?"

"The King himself gave it to us, Mr. Freemaster. He sent us to your town so that all his friends could see it and be encouraged."

"Well that's fine, except that most of his friends are in prison, and the rest of them are dead."

Theodora shuddered. Arlen sighed. "But why are they in prison? For what?"

"For gathering together. For singing. For mentioning the King."

"They put people in prison for things like that?"

"They murder people for less than that, son. This is a dangerous city."

"How can we show the book to as many of the King's friends as possible, Mr. Freemaster? That's what we're here for."

The man studied the children carefully. Did he dare trust them? He seemed about to say something, and then a frown crossed his brow. Theodora noticed the change in his expression. She put her hands in her pockets, and softly said, "Get out of here, whisperer! The King doesn't want you here!"

"Excuse me?" said Mr. Freemaster, who was evidently a little hard of hearing.

"Oh, excuse *me*, sir. I was just telling a rat to get out of the room!" Theodora glanced at Arlen, who rolled his eyes.

"Oh, I see. A rat. Lots of rats here. But back to your question, children. I am expecting a few of the King's friends to visit me this afternoon. Some of us still try to get together when we can. As far as I'm concerned, you are welcome to show the book to them if you wish."

Within a few minutes, as predicted, men and women began to arrive at Freemaster's door. Each entered the room alone, nodded politely to the others, and sat down cross-legged on the floor. There were eight of them by the time the last came in, and soon they were softly singing together.

> Our King is a glorious King,
> He shines like a beautiful star.
> He hears us when we speak to him,
> He sees us wherever we are.

They sang the song over and over. Then, one at a time, they spoke to the King out loud.

"I need health, Your Majesty. My child is sick."

"I need protection, Your Majesty. My husband is in prison."

"I need comfort, Your Majesty. My son has been killed."

"I need food, Your Majesty. I have not eaten for days."

After each request, everyone whispered, "The King knows. The King feels. The King understands."

Theodora kept her hand in her pocket, keeping an alert eye out for whisperers. After they had spoken, Mr. Freemaster introduced Arlen, who presented the book to the people. Instantly it came to life for them.

Then Theodora had an idea! Why not ask the King to provide a meal for everyone? She put her hand in her pocket. "King!" she murmured so that no one could hear, "Please send food for these poor people!"

All at once the table was covered with fruit, cheese, bread, and cups of milk. When the King's friends had finished studying the book, they were aglow with joy, and how their eyes shone to see the feast on the table!

Theodora was pleased that she'd thought to ask for a meal. Arlen was satisfied that he'd introduced the book properly. The people were smiling and even laughed softly among themselves. Everyone felt peace and hope and joy. Everyone felt the King's love in a new and special way.

And then, with a terrible crash, Mr. Freemaster's door was kicked in. Fear gripped the King's friends with cold, strangling fingers. They turned and peered into the hard faces of two dozen fierce warriors whose helmets glittered savagely in the twilight.

"An unlawful assembly! Stolen food! Association with a known traitor!" The officer in charge glared at Freemaster and barked out orders as he investigated the room with his eyes. "Arrest them! Chain them together!" The officer just missed seeing Arlen hide the book inside his shirt.

The abusive commander slapped food out of the starving people's hands.

He shoved them shivering and trembling, onto the floor.

He ordered them shackled, chained, and dragged away to the dungeon.

And as they went, weeping and hopeless, he and his warriors laughed heartily, helping themselves to the remaining food on the table.

8

Songs in the Darkness

ARLEN AND THEODORA'S legs were bloody and raw from being dragged through the streets of Mansfield. Heavy chains bruised their arms, fear weighed down their hearts—fear of hideous torture, unspeakable humiliation, even death.

Miraculously, Arlen had managed to hold on to the golden book the King had given them. At the moment, however, the King seemed little more than a remote dream, and a disappointing dream at that. Why had he let this happen?

Along with the other captured men and women, Arlen and Theodora were taken to a distant, rundown section of the town wall. The entrance to the dungeon amounted to little more than a steel door in the wall with two warriors standing guard beside it. Inside, a surly man recorded their names in a large, filthy book. Then they were shoved down a gloomy staircase.

Tears streamed down Theodora's face as she tumbled down the stone steps. "Stand up!" ordered the guard. She tried her best to scramble to her feet. "I said, stand up!"

Speechless with fear, the girl finally caught her balance just in time to hear a door creak open. She was pushed into a vast room. The sound of dripping water echoed in the darkness, as did the clanking of chains.

A uniformed woman led Theodora to an empty bed. She obediently stretched herself out on it, glad for the rest. Her legs were chained to the steel bed frame. She could hardly move them.

Theodora's eyes eventually became accustomed to the darkness, and she could see rows and rows of cots, a man or woman chained to each one. Hundreds and hundreds of prisoners populated the immense, foul-smelling room!

She lay very still, her heart pounding in her ears. The door creaked again, and then slammed. She held her breath. Squinting into the shadows, she could see movement. Arlen was being chained to the bed next to hers.

Just then a cracking voice spoke from another bed. "So you're one of the children who brought all the troubles to Mansfield. We've heard about you and your friend."

"What trouble did we bring? We brought a book from the King, that's all."

"You are a liar! You were sent as a spy. You've caused some of the King's best friends to be arrested."

Theodora was relieved to hear Arlen's angry voice. "If we're spies, then why are we in prison? We'd be free as birds if we were working for the prince."

The cracking voice answered bitterly, "The Prince is loyal to no one—not even to his spies. You are spies, and we know it. So don't try to fool us."

"We are friends of the King," Theodora persisted. "The King sent us here, and we were arrested along with his other friends. We love the King!"

"Don't we all. Don't we all," replied the cracking voice, which fell silent at last.

Hours passed in silence but for the clatter of chains, soft whispers, and the scuttling of rats. A thick feeling of depression pressed down against Arlen and Theodora's minds. They were unable to think clearly, and they had nothing whatsoever to say to each other. Vague fears passed through them in waves, and despair drove away any sense of hope. Time dragged by. They turned away several disgusting meals brought by their guards. Hours seemed like days. Or perhaps days had passed. How long had they been there by now?

At last Theodora managed to whisper, "Arlen, what are we going to do?"

Arlen paused for a long time and sighed deeply before he answered. "Well, I've been thinking about that. Theodora, we're going to show the book to the people in this dungeon. That's what we came for, and that's what we're going to do. Once our legs are free, there'll be no problem."

"But they all hate us! They already hate us."

"It's because of the whisperers. Once they see the book, they'll understand."

"And how will we get our legs free anyway, Arlen?"

"I don't know, but the King will help. We *need* our legs to walk around and show the book to the other prisoners. And he said he'd help us with our needs."

Theodora lay back on the stiff bed and tried to extend her legs. The chains were heavy, and the shackles rubbed against her ankles. "Oh, King..." She wanted to talk to him, but sadness filled her throat with sobs. "Oh, King..."

A sound caught her attention. It was the clanking of chains, and it was coming from Arlen's bed.

"What are you doing?" she whispered.

"I'm taking off my chains," he answered matter-of-factly.

She strained her eyes to peer through the gloom. Arlen was now sitting on the edge of the bed, rubbing his bare ankles with his hand.

"How...?"

"Shhh! I'm coming to help you now."

"How did you do it?"

"By asking the King for help and putting my hands in my pockets. Be quiet, Theodora, and I'll get your feet free, too."

Before long the two children were able to move about the dungeon, softly explaining to their fellow prisoners who they were and why they were there. Many of the men and women in the beds were desperately ill, and all of them were terribly thin.

The whisperers had obviously preceded them, because most of the convicts honestly believed that Arlen and Theodora were spies. Once they saw the book, however, they began to change their minds.

The room was so filthy and the smell so foul that no guards actually stayed inside. Such a close guard would have been unnecessary anyway, considering that fact that every prisoner was chained. Everyone, that is, except for Arlen and Theodora.

Each day they awoke with their feet shoved through

their shackles to make the guards think that their chains were still intact. After their sickening breakfast of dry bread soaked in rancid oil was brought in, the children carefully tiptoed around the room, showing the book to all who wanted to see it.

Theodora kept a sharp eye out for whisperers and guards. Arlen often used his pockets to provide medicine for the most seriously ill, and he often gave them food and drink as well. Gradually the prisoners began to trust the children. Some of them related stories about how they'd come to be arrested.

"Everyone in this room is here because of the King," one forlorn woman explained. "Take me, for example. A group of the King's friends were meeting in my home. My own son called in the warriors and had us all arrested. He wants to be a warrior himself because of all the special privileges they have in our township." The woman began to weep. "My own son. Can you believe it?"

Another woman pointed to the King as the golden book was opened before her. "He's been here, you know. He's walked around here and talked to us. I didn't know who he was, but now I recognize his face."

"You mean he's visited you here in the dungeon?"

"I've been here for ten years, and I think he's come to see us at least once a year. He encouraged us and urged us to be patient just a little longer. We thought he was a kind foreigner on a diplomatic mission."

Two young men were chained side by side in a far

corner of the room. "We were thrown in here because we used to sing about the King in our house. The next-door neighbors reported us. At least we think that's how we were arrested. I've never been sure."

"Do you know about the whisperers?" Arlen asked.

The young man shook his head. "What do you mean?"

"Whisperers are invisible little creatures that whisper lies into people's ears. We think they act as spies for the prince, too. Don't you think so, Theodora?"

She nodded. "How else would the prince know what people do in their own homes? Of course they're spies. But tell me, do you remember any of the songs you used to sing about the King?"

"Of course we remember them. But we wouldn't want to sing them here. We'd be killed if anyone heard us!"

"Could you teach me one of the songs? Sing it softly, just for me? Please?"

The young man's hollow eyes searched Theodora's face. What did he have to lose? Besides, he really missed singing. He really did. Softly, his voice husky with emotion, he began to sing,

> Dear King, how you love us,
> Know us, feel, and understand.

Dear King, how you care for us,
Lead us gently by the hand.

Dear King, how we love you!
Help us prove our love is true.
Dear King, can you hear our song?
Can you feel our love for you?

As the young man sang for Theodora, a gentle murmur rippled about the room. It was very faint, but it sounded like music. Who was singing? Theodora glanced about in wonder. It was the prisoners! One by one, their voices raspy and feeble, they were joining in the song: "Dear King, how you love us..."

Before long, the room was filled with melody, and the music grew stronger with every word. Another song began, and then another. Onward and outward the music drifted. It resounded in the fetid cell. It passed through the city walls. It reached across the night sky and beyond.

Far away, in his castle, the King heard the singing. His eyes filled with tears as he thought about the prisoners in Mansfield. This was the year he had set aside for their deliverance, but the appointed month and week and day had not yet arrived. His Mansfield friends knew nothing of his rescue plans anyway. They fully expected to die in their terrible bondage. And still they sang about loving him!

The King stood up. He angrily pounded his fist against the desk where he had been sitting. The people of

Mansfield had suffered terribly on his behalf, and he would not wait another moment to help them! He summoned his messengers and gave them instructions. Then he urgently left the castle. Enough was enough!

Meanwhile, as the prisoners sang, they noticed that the chains around their feet were growing looser and looser. And as the music grew louder, the room seemed to grow brighter. Sick men and women began to feel better. Angry prisoners began to feel a sense of peace. Arlen and Theodora looked at each other in amazement. What was happening?

Just then a warrior burst into the room, his face florid with rage. "What do you think you're doing?"

"Why, we're singing, sir."

"You are supposed to be silent here. Singing is not permitted!"

The room fell silent. Then, somewhere in a distant corner, another song began. The warrior stalked toward the ones who started it and slapped their faces. But soon others had joined them, and even though his palm bruised various cheeks and chins, everyone kept on singing.

Another warrior appeared. Still the song continued. By now the prisoner's voices were loud and strong and joyful. More warriors entered the room. They could see that nothing would stop the singing. Nothing but death.

"Take them to the Prince!" commanded a senior officer who had been summoned by his nervous underlings. "Unshackle them, and take them to Prince Newcastle immediately!"

And so it was that an immense, ragged choir went marching down the streets of Mansfield, singing as it went. Whips cut into the prisoner's backs and legs. Blows stung their faces and heads. Yet still they sang, more triumphantly with every step.

They marched toward Prince Newcastle's palace. They ascended its ornate stairway and crossed its fabulous, richly colored carpet. Barefoot, with bloody wounds, and with pathetic strips of clothing hanging from their bony shoulders, they headed fearlessly into the great hall. The songs had given them courage. They were prepared to die with praise for the King on their lips!

The doors to the throne room were thrown open. Hundreds of wretched captives surged forward, resolutely prepared to encounter the scowling presence of Prince Newcastle himself. He was the heartless tyrant who had kept them locked in poverty. He was the cruel dictator who had made their lives a nightmare of fear and desperation. He was the bloodthirsty killer who would most certainly sentence them to death.

Our King is a glorious king!
He shines like a beautiful star...

The song rose in a mighty swell. And as the prisoners bravely looked up, determined to face their tormentor, they saw something impossible. Something inconceivable. Something beyond their wildest dreams.

Prince Newcastle was not on the throne. None of his henchman were anywhere to be seen. The warriors were all gone.

Standing before them in a pure white robe was the glorious King himself!

The people stopped their song and rubbed their eyes. Then they began again, and they sang as they'd never sung before!

Once the joyful concert was finished and several minutes of thunderous applause had quieted, the King made a proclamation.

"Prince Newcastle is gone forever!" he announced. "I have removed him and all his evil followers from the township. Your music has touched my heart and set you free! You may return in peace to your homes and families. My messengers will quickly provide you with food and clothes. Your lives will be worth living again, I promise you."

There was more prolonged applause and cheering. Then the people looked around, wondering whether they should stay or rush out to find their friends and loved ones.

The King spoke again. "Just a moment. Before you go, I want to honor my special friends, Arlen and Theodora. I know how much they have meant to you, and I want you to be able to thank them before they go. Children, where are you?"

Everyone paused, looked around, called out. "Arlen? Theodora? Are you here?"

But the two children from Place-Beneath-the-Castle were nowhere to be found.

9

Empty Pockets

BESIDE A ROADWAY, under a broad oak tree, sat the two children. Their clothes, so carefully sewn by Mr. Weatherworth, were ripped to shreds. Their hands and faces were covered with dirt and bleeding scratches. They were hungry and thirsty. They were cold and weary beyond belief.

But the worst pain the two children felt was the devastation in their hearts.

"The book is gone. I've lost the King's beautiful

book. It's gone. It's gone!" Arlen repeated the words over and over to himself. He was unable even to cry, so great was his sorrow. "I've lost the book. And it's your fault, Theodora!"

"It's your fault, too!" she spat back at him. But Theodora was submerged in her own misery. She had disobeyed the King. In fact, she had done exactly what he'd told her *not* to do.

"It's not a good idea to begin a task for me and to then turn back," he had once cautioned her. Yet Theodora had run away from her responsibilities at the most crucial moment, in the midst of a dangerous situation. Even worse, she had encouraged Arlen to run with her, and he had lost the King's book in the process.

Guilt, shame, and mistrust filled both children's minds as they sat beside the road. They blamed themselves. They blamed each other. Again and again they tried to sort out what had happened just a few hours before.

They had been singing along with all the other prisoners in the dungeon. Warriors had come in and tried to stop them, but they'd sung on fearlessly. A senior officer had ordered all the convicts to be taken before Prince Newcastle and had removed their shackles. The children had been marching along the Mansfield streets with everyone else, heading toward the palace.

And that's when everything in their memories began to blur.

Theodora remembered being seized by sudden panic. All at once she had believed, beyond a shadow of doubt, that she was going to be killed. She had looked from side to side and had noticed a workman's ladder leaning against the city wall. *Escape!* The word had leapt to her mind. *Go up the ladder and escape!*

"Arlen, look!" she'd called to her friend, pointing to the ladder.

Arlen remembered being frightened, too. He had suddenly found himself doubting the King's authority. *He is not as strong as you think.* The warning had echoed through his mind. "He is unable to help you now."

"Escape!" Theodora had urged him at that very moment. "Let's go up the ladder and escape!"

The two children had clambered up the ladder in sheer terror, sure they were being followed. Reaching the top of the wall, they had confronted a thorny hedge as tall as they were. By then they'd had no choice but to find a way over it.

Thorns had cut into their hands and faces and torn their clothes into ragged strips. But eventually they had reached the other side, where they had scurried along the wall until they came to a tree. Then they had climbed down its branches, jumped to the ground, and raced along the highway until the Mansfield wall was almost out of view behind them.

And as for the book? Neither of them could recall

dropping it or hearing it fall to the ground. But somehow the golden volume had vanished.

Darkness was falling across the land, and a pale strip of pink was all that remained of the sunset. Arlen and Theodora drifted into sleep for a few minutes at a time, but so terrible were their dreams that they awoke in dismay again and again. Neither could find a single encouraging word to say to the other.

A fine arc of a moon began to rise in the twilight sky, and the moon always reminded Theodora of the King. How many times had she looked out of her window at home to see his far-off castle glimmering in the moonlight? She could not bear to think of him now, so great was her grief. Still, as the moon rose, a slender hope tried to light her inner darkness.

Pockets...

Her answering thoughts were of hopelessness. *He won't help me now because I failed him. I can't ask him for help when I haven't obeyed.*

Pockets... The word occurred to her again. She sighed and pretended she hadn't heard.

At the same time, Arlen wrestled with his own anguish. He was painfully hungry, and thirst burned in his throat.

Pockets... the boy thought. But he, too, set the idea aside.

I don't want to ask the King for help because I've lost his book.

All night long the children struggled—sleepless, starving, sick at heart. Ugly criticisms of each other persisted. Doubts about the King continued. The night was cold, and the weaver's wonderful clothes were too ripped to warm them. Still, now and then, a single word seemed to burst like an iridescent bubble in their minds.

Pockets...

At last, just before daybreak, Theodora sat up, found what was left of her pockets, put her hands inside, and spoke but one sentence. "I'm sorry, King." Tears drenched her face.

Arlen stirred and looked at her in anger. "Stop feeling sorry for yourself!" he snapped.

"I am not feeling sorry for myself! I'm feeling sorry for what I've done."

The boy withdrew in silence, not sure whether to believe her or not.

Just then, the two children noticed a party of travelers advancing toward them. They glanced around for a place to hide, not wanting anyone to see them in their wretched condition. But before they could move their sore bodies out of the way, someone cried out, "Arlen! Theodora!"

It was Duncan from King's Common! With him was his mother, Rose, and all the people who had gathered at their home to see the book about the King. Several new faces were in the group, too.

The children looked at the King's Common villagers and immediately realized that they were no longer attired in purple. The men wore simple green tunics and trousers; the women wore graceful blue dresses, with flowers in their hair. And their smiles shone far brighter than any of the foolish crowns they'd given up not many days before.

"The King's rainbow messengers came last night and carried us out of the village, past the gate. We're on our way to our new home at Castlerock! But what on earth has happened to you?"

"We're just resting..." Arlen bit his lip, not wanting to talk about their plight.

"We're waiting for the King," Theodora said, wishing with all her heart that it were true.

Duncan seemed rushed, eager to carry out orders of his own. "Well, we can't stay long, but I'm so glad we got a chance to see you. If it hadn't been for you and your willingness to bring the golden book to King's Common, we would have never been freed! You were so courageous and so obedient to the King that you made us brave, too."

Arlen and Theodora looked at each other in disbelief. Brave? Obedient? That certainly wasn't the way the saw themselves at the moment! Nevertheless, the former citizens of King's Common gratefully embraced them as they said good-bye.

As they continued their trek, leaving the two children behind, Duncan and his friends passed a solitary man who walked toward Arlen and Theodora from the opposite direction. The travelers paid him little mind. The children could not see him, because he was approaching them from behind. But they were in his full view, and this is what he saw.

Two pitiful children sat in rags beside the roadway, under a broad oak tree. And swarming over their laps and shoulders and heads were the most repulsive creatures imaginable. Dozens of the ratlike animals slithered about, climbing and crawling all over the boy and girl.

At the sight of the children and the creatures, the man began to run toward them.

The first thing the children heard was his voice. "Get away from my children! Go, and die!"

The first thing the children felt was a sense of immense relief, as if they were awakening from a horrible nightmare. And then, the next thing they knew, the King himself was reaching down, enfolding them in his arms. He touched healing ointment to their bleeding faces and hands. He gave them a drink from his bottle with the silvery cap. He wiped away their tears and dried a few of his own in the process.

Then, without a word, he showed them a book he'd been carrying with him. Its golden cover was dented. Some of its pages were bent and soiled. But the title, *Tales of the King*, was clearly legible on the cover. And not a single, living word had been lost.

"Where did you find it?" Arlen murmured, unable to look into the King's sympathetic eyes.

"One of the townspeople found it at the bottom of a ladder. It's all right, Arlen. I'll keep it for now."

Theodora was so overcome with guilt that she couldn't face either Arlen or the King. "It was my fault. We were singing, and everything was fine. Then, all of a sudden, I thought we were going to be killed! I panicked and tried to escape. And I talked Arlen into coming with me."

Arlen spoke up immediately. "I was fine, too, singing and marching toward the palace. Then, all at once I began to doubt you! I feel so foolish now, but at the time I was terrified."

Theodora nodded. "It was so strange! We went from happy to sad, from trusting to terrified, in just a matter of seconds. Everything went wrong! I'm so sorry..." She began to cry again.

"Don't you see what happened, children?"

The boy and girl looked at each other blankly. "What do you mean?"

"Well, I'll give you a hint. When I walked up to you today, what was the first thing I said?"

Theodora could still hear his forceful words. "You said, 'Get away from my children!' "

"And who do you think I was talking to?"

Suddenly a light began to dawn in Arlen's tired,

blue eyes. "Whisperers! They must have attacked us while we were marching with the choir."

The King nodded and began to tell his own story.

He had heard the prisoners' song in his castle and had determined to rescue them right then. After arriving in Mansfield, his rainbow messengers had immediately seized Prince Newcastle, his political advisers, and his warriors. All the corrupt leaders had been dispatched to the King's own dungeon, far beneath the foundations of the castle.

Then, having rid the township of its evil leadership, the King had begun to take food, drink, and clothes to the village people, all the while awaiting the dungeon choir's arrival at the palace. But everywhere he went, the whisperers had slowed his work and caused continuous confusion.

And so, with one mighty order, he had commanded all the whisperers to leave Mansfield and drown themselves in a nearby swamp. They had no choice but to obey his authority. But a vengeful hoard of the creatures had evidently leaped upon Arlen and Theodora, delaying their own fate by tormenting the two children with thoughts of doubt and fear and death.

"We should have known," Theodora was starting to find fault with herself again. "It was so easy to watch out for whisperers lying to other people. I never once thought about their attacking us!"

"Neither did I," agreed Arlen. "I guess we thought they'd leave us alone."

The King shook his head emphatically. "You can never be too alert, children. Evil attacks will always be most successful when you are unprepared for them. But enough of that. Don't you think it's time we returned to the castle?"

Arlen and Theodora tried to stand up, but their trembling legs would not support them. The children reeled from dizziness, exhaustion, and pain. Fortunately, they didn't have to take a single step.

Moments later, a warm wind lifted their hair as they streaked through the sky in the arms of a rainbow being. They could hardly keep their eyes open to see the panorama of villages and townships and cities outstretched below them. They didn't even recognize their own cottages in Place-Beneath-the-Castle, although they flew directly over their roofs.

Next thing they knew, they had arrived at the castle and were being tenderly bathed in hot, fragrant waters. After a nourishing meal from the King's own table, they were gently tucked into soft, downy beds. At last, they slept.

And when Arlen and Theodora awoke, a new awareness filled their minds with warm, golden peace. The King loved them far more than they had realized!

It didn't matter whether they had failed or succeeded; whether they wore royal purple or rags;

whether they were well or wounded, happy or hurting, near or far away.

The King really, really loved them! He always had. He always would.

As far as Arlen and Theodora were concerned, that's all they needed to know.

10

Puzzles and a Promise

MORNING AT THE CASTLE
arrived with caroling birds, a soft breeze, and an
invitation to share breakfast with the King. Arlen and
Theodora sat with him at an outdoor table, surrounded
by a dazzling array of flowers.

Clouds filled some of the valleys below them with
soft, white billows. Here and there they could see a patch
of green or a silvery ribbon of river or a cluster of
cottages. The troubles of King's Common and Mansfield

seemed an eternity away, considering the delectable fare the three friends were now enjoying, the pleasing company, and the freshness of the air.

Arlen and Theodora looked very unlike the wretched waifs the King had rescued just the day before. Their hair, clean and brushed, gleamed in the early sunlight. Their scratched faces were nearly healed. Best of all, their smiles had returned. In fact, they had never felt more contented.

"Since yesterday was so miserable for you, I have some surprises for you today," the King began, a twinkle in his eyes.

"Surprises?" Both children spoke at the same time. "For us?"

The King nodded. "First of all, Theodora, I know how much you enjoy puzzles. You've always tried to solve them in your mind, and sometimes you've worked on picture puzzles with your sisters and brothers, haven't you?"

"I *love* puzzles!" she replied. "But how did you know?"

"Of course I know you love puzzles. And puzzles are part of my surprise for you. But as for you, Arlen..."

"What kind of a puzzle is it?" Theodora put her hand on the King's arm, hoping for more information. But he shook his head. "Oh, no, Theodora. If I tell you any more, it's sure to spoil the fun. And as for you Arlen, how do you feel about maps, son?"

Arlen grinned broadly. "You *know* how I feel about

maps, sir. I could spend hours, even days, studying maps. Granma says I'm a rather good mapmaker myself!"

"Hmmm. Well then, I suppose your surprise will have to involve maps of some sort. Let's see. I wonder what I could do about maps..."

The children glanced at each other, merriment and mischief dancing across their faces. They knew very well that the King had already planned every aspect of their surprises. He was just teasing them with his talk of puzzles and maps. But what was he going to do, really?

After breakfast, the King took them on a joyous walk. At the end of the path stood a greenhouse with a crystalline roof. Shining so brilliantly in the sunlight, it might well have been constructed of diamonds.

They entered the greenhouse through an elegantly etched door. "Come sit down for a few minutes, children." Arlen and Theodora seated themselves in soft, comfortable chairs and looked around. Glass walls enclosed a miniature country landscape rich in meadows, orchards, streams, and ponds.

"This is my waiting room," the King explained, heading toward the door. "Wait for me here until I get back."

It was exceptionally quiet in the waiting room. The children sat very still for awhile, enjoying the soothing sound of the brooks and the fragrance of the outdoors. But before long they grew a little restless.

"I wonder how long he'll be gone. Did he say where

he was going? Do you think it would be all right for us to walk around?" Theodora whispered, unsure of the waiting-room rules.

"He didn't say we couldn't," Arlen replied. The boy was rather bored, wishing the King would hurry back with his map surprise.

The children walked around and studied the diminutive landscape carefully. Although it was early winter in their part of the kingdom, it seemed to be springtime inside the greenhouse. "Look," Theodora exclaimed suddenly. "Did you notice those tiny crocuses before?"

"They weren't there before. Nothing was there but grass."

"That's just what I thought," the girl replied. "And look at the orchard! There are buds on the little fruit trees and new leaves on the saplings. They weren't there either, I'm nearly sure. I never saw them forming. Did you?"

Arlen shook his head in amazement. "Look at the meadow. All of a sudden it's full of wildflowers! Let's sit down again, Theodora. I think we need to watch all of this more carefully.

They returned to their chairs. In the seconds or minutes or hours that followed, the landscape passed swiftly through one season and into the next. Pale buds blossomed into a confetti of cherry blossoms. Flowers transformed into fruit. Flowers of every hue sprang from the soil. Trees gradually changed from rich summer green into brilliant shades of gold and crimson, then faded to brown. Once the dry leaves blew away, icicles glittered on branches, and ponds froze into green glass. Then, before the children knew it, spring had returned again, and then summer and fall.

They waited. They watched. They paced around. They stood and sat and fidgeted. Where was the King? When would he be back? Had he forgotten them? Why had he left them there?

Judging by the changing seasons in the greenhouse, several years seemed to have gone by. Yet Arlen and Theodora knew it really hadn't been long at all since the King left. And then, just when they were least expecting him, he reappeared.

"Did you notice," he asked pleasantly, "how many beautiful things can take place while you're waiting?"

"Oh, we noticed, all right. But we weren't feeling very patient, I'm afraid." Arlen, more than ready to go, was already headed toward the door.

The King nodded. "Waiting always requires patience. But in my kingdom, waiting time is never wasted. And I'm never late, either!"

The children were very quiet for a moment. Then Theodora softly asked, "And what about the puzzle?"

"Oh, that's right! Let's take a look at the puzzle room."

"The puzzle *room*? Do you mean a roomful of

puzzles?" By now Theodora was walking backward, facing the King, trying to make him tell her more.

"One puzzle and one room, child. And here we are." The King, Arlen, and Theodora had entered the castle, turned down a hallway, and walked into a colossal chamber that seemed to go on forever. In the center of the room, a table extended beyond sight in both directions. And on the table sat an enormous puzzle, a mosaic of tiny pieces that created a vibrant and exquisite picture.

"What is it? What's the picture?" No matter how far nor how quickly Theodora walked, she couldn't reach either end of the table. Nor could she possibly see the entire puzzle at once.

"Come here." The King took the girl's hand. "This is the best way for me to explain. This is your part of the picture, Theodora. Do you recognize anything?"

There, right before her eyes, Theodora saw her life—as a baby, as a tot, as a growing child. She observed the many months she'd searched for the King. She discovered the day when she'd found him. Every moment of her life was represented in the puzzle. Still, it seemed that a number of pieces were missing.

"The missing pieces will show up later," explained the King. "Once you come to my castle at the end of your life in the kingdom, the picture will be complete. But even now, I can show you some things you may find interesting."

Theodora was breathless with fascination. "Look! There's the day my favorite auntie went away! I was just three, and she'd always lived with us. Then all of a sudden she was gone forever."

The King pointed to another part of the puzzle. "But there your auntie is! You see? She's part of the picture over here now."

"That's my cousin Maribelle."

"Yes, now you're looking at Maribelle's life. After her mother died, your auntie went to live with her. She became a sort of second mother to a lonely little girl.

"But look—back to your part of the puzzle. Here's that special doll you lost. Remember? Now she's in the arms of a poor child who'd never had a doll before. And here's the day your feelings were so badly hurt..."

The King continued to point out episodes in Theodora's past that she had never before understood—strange experiences, disappointments, unexplained occurrences. Somehow they all seemed to fit together.

"In my kingdom, all the events in your life work out for your very best, Theodora. You can't always see how until the picture is finished. But no piece of the puzzle is ever lost. And nothing ever happens without a reason."

Arlen's puzzle picture was incomplete, too. But he learned how his unloving parents had caused him to love the King better. He saw that his lonely childhood had made him a dearer friend to Theodora. He understood how his strict, stern tutor had helped him follow the King's instructions more carefully.

"But what about the maps?" Arlen looked at the King inquisitively, wondering what would happen next.

"Ah, yes. The maps. I'd nearly forgotten!"

"No you hadn't, sir. And neither had I!"

The King took each child's hand and led them down several hallways into the promised map room. The room's walls were hung with perfectly drawn and delicately painted maps of the kingdom. But these maps were most certainly unlike anything the children had ever seen before!

The King's maps were overlaid with a vivid network of brilliantly colored lines that were forever changing directions and pulsating with energy! They looked like tiny, living beams of colored light.

Arlen searched the walls until he found a part of the kingdom he recognized.

"That's right, Arlen." The King watched the boy approvingly. "That's Place-Beneath-the-Castle, Kingsdale, and the City of Bells."

"But sir, look at all these colored lines—blue and purple and green and red and yellow. They keep moving and vibrating and starting and stopping again. What are they? There are no pathways or roads between any of these places."

The King watched Arlen with amusement,

wondering if the boy would figure out the mystery without being told. "And what about the golden lines that lead to my castle?" he asked innocently.

Arlen studied the map and scratched his chin, trying to concentrate. "Hmmm...there's a red line from Granma's cottage to Theodora's cottage. But now its changing! Now there's a blue line from Granma's cottage to my father's house in the City of Bells. Look! Now there are two golden lines to the castle from Granma's!"

"Arlen," the King explained, "the lines are loving thoughts, not footpaths or roadways."

"Loving thoughts?"

The King knelt down and pulled the children close to him. "My kingdom has a name you've never yet heard. It's called the Kingdom of Love. Yes, it's a country you can see, made up of real villages, towns, and cities. But its true geography, history, and language is based on loving thoughts, loving deeds, and loving words."

"I don't understand, Your Majesty. You still have to have roadways..."

"Only for your feet, son. Your heart and mind can reach out to anyone, anytime, anywhere. When you think a loving thought about someone, no matter how far away he is, you build a pathway of love directly into his heart."

"So that's what the colors are for?"

"The deeper the love, the warmer the colors."

"And what about the golden lines coming and going from your castle?"

"Well, sometimes you ask me to do something special for people you love, don't you? I always reach out to them, whenever you ask. When that happens, your love touches them with warm, bright colors. And my love touches them with gold."

Needless to say, Arlen spent the better part of the afternoon in the map room. And by evening both children had more to think about than they could have ever imagined.

"So what have you learned today, Theodora?" The King looked at the little girl affectionately as the three friends sat by a fireplace after dinner.

"Well, I think I've learned three things. I've learned about waiting...and about trusting...and about loving thoughts."

The King nodded, and no one spoke for a while.

"Well, children," he said at last after stirring the fire, "You'll need to remember those three lessons the next time you take *Tales of the King* out into the kingdom. And, by the way, it's nearly time for you to go home again. I'm going to give you back the book tomorrow morning."

Arlen looked at Theodora a bit sheepishly and took a deep breath. Obviously, the King still trusted them with his golden book!

"And I'm going to send you away with a promise."

The children's eyes glowed. "What is the promise, Your Majesty?"

"Shouldn't it wait till tomorrow?"

"Oh, no!" the children cried out. "Tell us now! Tell us the promise now."

"All right, all right," the King said, smiling quietly. "The promise is simply this: *Our best adventures together are yet to come.*"

Once in his castle bed, Arlen tried to imagine what could possibly be better than the time he and Theodora had already spent with the King. Excitement surged through him. He contemplated the maps and the puzzles and the changing seasons.

Meanwhile, Theodora remembered the gentle way the King had smiled at them when he'd made his promise. Her heart stirred with love and joy. And she thought. And she dreamed. And she wondered.

About the Author

Lela Gilbert is a freelance writer living in Southern California. An author, collaborator, and ghostwriter, she has written or cowritten more than thirty published books since 1985. She also writes poetry and music.

Along with her writing assignments, she participates in several ongoing humanitarian projects, including her work and travels with the African Children's Choir. She has two sons, Dylan David and Colin Keith, and attends St. James Episcopal Church in Newport Beach, California.